DON'T MISS OUT ON ANY OF

SPARKNOTES®
SAT VOCABULARY NOVELS

BUSTED

HEAD OVER HEELS

RAVE NEW WORLD

SUN-KISSED

VAMPIRE DREAMS

Vam

Dre

pire

ams

AN SAT VOCABULARY NOVEL

BY TYCHE

Spark Publishing
A Division of Barnes & Noble Publishing
120 Fifth Avenue
New York, NY 10011
www.sparknotes.com

ISBN-13: 978-1-4114-0083-2
ISBN-10: 1-4114-0083-6

Please submit all questions or comments or report errors to
www.sparknotes.com/errors

Library of Congress Cataloging-in-Publication Data
Tyche.
Vampire dreams / by Tyche.
p. cm. — (SAT vocabulary novels)
Summary: Twenty-two-year-old James Weston, a medical student in London, is the victim of an apparent mugging that will change his life forever.
ISBN 1-4114-0083-6
[1. Vampires—Fiction.] I. Title. II. Series.
PZ7.T9355Vam 2004
[Fic]—dc22 2003028316

Printed and bound in the United States

PART I

Chapter One

James Weston hitched his black messenger bag higher on his shoulder and breathed in the crisp fall air. He always felt **jubilant** at the beginning of a new term, something about the new possibilities and opportunities that come with a clean slate. Plus he had just left Mr. Morrow's class on **hematology**—the study of blood—and he could already tell it was going to be great. The subject seemed so cool, and James loved **taciturn** old Mr. Morrow himself. Other students **railed** against the strict structure of the class and tough content, but James was ready for a good challenge. And he was totally in **awe** of Mr. Morrow's brilliance. James knew that he could learn a lot from someone who was such an **authority**.

"'Lo, James!" A golden-haired girl in a roll-neck sweater and low-slung corduroys waved to him from across the quad.

James felt his cheeks warm up at the sight of Patty Griggs. His heart always seemed to thump a couple of extra beats whenever she was around. Too bad he didn't have any time to hang out right now. His mother took dinnertime really seriously. Actually, she took *everything* seriously.

"'Lo, Patty!" James called back, slowing his stride a bit.

"Where are you off to, then?" Patty shouted.

"Late for dinner!"

Patty grinned. "Don't want to upset Mum?"

"Right!" James waved and hurried on. He hoped Patty would get why he had to rush. She still lived with her parents, too. Most of the students at Wilcox University did, actually. Only the other parents didn't seem quite as . . . *intense* as James's mum.

Leaves crunched underfoot as James strode down the narrow

jubilant: joyful or triumphant
hematology: study of blood or blood-forming organs
taciturn: silent or reserved
railed: complained angrily
awe: admiration or wonder
authority: expert

path that led across the quadrangle at the center of the university. The late afternoon sunlight shone orange on the red brick of the **hallowed** buildings, and James felt the same light on his face, warming his skin. James was in his last year of medical school at Wilcox, and he knew he would miss the place when the year was over. All of the **quaint** buildings and customs of the place held a special spot in his heart. Still, part of him couldn't wait. He was twenty-two years old and excited to get started as a real doctor. James already knew exactly what he would do first. His plan was to start out working for an international relief agency, helping people in need. This was not just because of his **magnanimous** nature, although James liked to think that was a major factor. The truth was, James also really wanted to travel and see the world—and maybe get a little distance from his mum, too. As much as he loved her, it was hard sometimes knowing his mum was different from other people's parents, always having to live his life around her weird schedule and habits. He knew a lot of people out there would probably find the idea of embarking on a medical career in a foreign place **daunting**, but to James it seemed like the perfect opportunity to take his life in a new direction.

James smiled and nodded as he passed a couple of guys he knew from one of his classes and quickened his step as he left the campus. He had promised his mother that he would be home in time for dinner, and for Angelica Weston, the dinner hour was **sacrosanct**. It was a pretty long walk from campus to his home, but James could make it in twenty minutes if he hurried. The streets around him were tranquil, the locals packed into the **ubiquitous** pubs for their evening meals and ale. James found the silence comforting, and he allowed himself to fall into an almost trancelike state as he listened to the **cadence** of his breathing and his own footsteps.

The streets in this section of London were cobblestoned, and James kept to the far right, where the stones were more even, worn

hallowed: sacred or respected
quaint: old-fashioned or charming
magnanimous: generous
daunting: overwhelming or frightening
sacrosanct: holy or untouchable
ubiquitous: ever present
cadence: rhythm

smooth by centuries of foot traffic. Neon signs advertising Guinness beer glowed from dark pub windows, mingling with the light of old-fashioned gas lamps and the strange, purple twilight to guide James's way. James loved that about London—the sense of being in a present that was firmly lodged in history. Everywhere you went, thousands of people had been there before.

James was so involved with his thoughts that he hardly noticed a couple of men as he passed. They were standing beneath an awning, dressed in carpenter jeans and heavy work boots, talking in low voices as James passed. While the gentle melody of an old **ballad** wafted from the pub behind them, the door opened and a third man stepped out. James walked on, his mind still on hematology.

Suddenly the sound of heavy footsteps pounded behind him. James turned and saw one of the men running toward him, the others right behind. Too late, James saw the alley beside him, took in the hard expressions on the men's faces, and heard their determined breathing. *They're going to rob me,* James thought just as the first man caught him by the arm and dragged him into the alley.

"Give us your money, and we won't give you nae trouble," the man said, breathing **rancid** air into James's face. His eyebrows were thick and dark over flashing black eyes, and his body was short and square—solidly built. By then the other men had come up behind him, and James could see that they were as strong as the first man, built like oxen. One was over a head taller than the others—almost a giant—and the third had fair hair and the kind of thick neck that comes from bodybuilding. "Give it over!" the first man shouted again, shaking James by the shoulders.

It took only a moment for every **hackneyed** scene in every cheap television drama he had ever watched to flash through James's mind. In all of them the hero either handed over the money or used martial arts to overpower his attackers. James's mind **vacillated** be-

ballad: love song or other simple song
rancid: rotten

hackneyed: worn out or clichéd

vacillated: moved back and forth

tween his two options. James didn't know any martial arts. Besides, he was small, and even if he knew karate, he wasn't sure that he could overpower three attackers who were bigger than he was. James had been slight all of his life. A severe lung infection when he was a boy had left him weak, unable to be much of an athlete. This was part of the reason that he found his **nascent** powers as an academic—when the other children were outside playing football or cricket, James was inside, reading.

Still, James **balked** at the idea of handing over money to three thugs. Things had been this way his whole life—the bigger, stronger kids thought that they had the right to overpower him just because they could. And now a white-hot fury burned in James's chest—anger at his own stupidity and lack of strength.

The tall thug reached over and poked James in the chest. "Don't be stupid," he warned.

Suddenly James's rage spilled over. "If you want my money, you'll have to come and take it," he spat. He paused a moment, then added, "You **vacuous** thug." He wasn't sure why he did it. He knew that he should have tried to be **pacific**, to get the thugs to leave him alone, but no—he'd had to provoke them. Maybe he wanted to lash out the only way he knew how—with words. James had never been **garrulous**. On the contrary, he knew how to choose his words carefully and strike where his enemy was weakest.

Predictably, the thugs took **umbrage** at the insult they didn't understand. The man with the heavy eyebrows grabbed James's collar and began to twist it as the tall thug pounded the side of James's head, making his ears ring. The third stood back and pulled something from his pocket. It gleamed silver in the light of a streetlamp—a switchblade knife.

"Give it over," Heavy Eyebrows demanded. "Or I'll use me flip knife to carve you a new face."

James's pulse raced from fear as he realized he'd been sucked

nascent: budding
balked: stopped short; refused to
vacuous: stupid
pacific: peacemaking or diplomatic
garrulous: wordy
umbrage: offense

into a **quagmire** with no escape. His **façade** of bravery fell away as he sank toward the ground, wincing in pain. *Just give them the money,* he told himself, but he couldn't make himself do it. He wouldn't **abase** himself that way. "No," James choked out as bursts of color flashed across his eyes. He couldn't breathe—he wasn't getting enough air. Heavy Eyebrows twisted his shirt collar harder.

The thug with the knife lunged toward him, and James found himself at the center of a **maelstrom** as he struggled to free his body while the three thugs pulled him back. Pain exploded across his gut, and the air was knocked from him. Agony screamed across his left cheekbone. James lashed out, but his fists fell against empty air. He slumped to the ground as blows thundered across his body. The thugs seemed to grow more **zealous** with every strike, brutalizing James with a ferocity coming from some **feral**, savage place inside them.

He tried to use his messenger bag as a shield, but Heavy Eyebrows slit the strap with his knife and yanked away the bag. He gave James a sharp kick with his lug-soled boot, followed by another. Another pulled his wallet from his back pocket. James couldn't see which one did it—his eyes were swollen shut. The blows began to **wane**, then stopped altogether.

"Many thanks for the contribution," said a mocking, **saccharine** voice. Then the sound of footsteps padding away, and James was alone.

James lay half submerged in a mud puddle, the uneven cobblestones jabbing into his back, gasping for air. His mind was working quickly, **fabricating** a million ways that he could take revenge on the three thugs. He wanted to hurt them, to torture them, to get back at them for what they had done to him. It wasn't just the pain they had caused him—it was the humiliation. James **wallowed** in the violence of his emotions until they reached a **zenith** of frustration. Then he forced himself to breathe deeply, to control his lungs

quagmire: sticky situation
abase: humiliate
façade: flimsy appearance
maelstrom: violent storm
zealous: eager
feral: wild or untamed
wane: lessen
saccharine: overly and falsely sweet
fabricating: making up
wallowed: indulged in excessively
zenith: high point

like he used to do when he was a child and the doctor would come and test his breath. Finally James's **respiration** returned to normal, and he hauled himself to his feet, his clothes a dripping, muddy, bloody mess. He was pretty sure that none of his bones were broken, but his cheek was bleeding profusely.

James had to hold one eye open as he staggered into the cool fall night.

* * * * *

James lurched in through the front door of his house, squinting at the light cast from the chandelier hanging from the ceiling in the hallway. James's mother had **eclectic** taste, and it showed in the furnishings of their town house, which felt like some museum from the past. Still, although Angelica's decorating was a bit **idiosyncratic**, her guests often said the place was "unexpectedly **elegant**." Balinese wood carvings stood beside Louis XIV chairs, each complementing the other with their dark wood and excellent craftsmanship. James had always avoided bringing his own friends back home. He was pretty sure they wouldn't be talking about the elegance of the furniture—they'd just be freaked at how old-fashioned everything was.

James reeled into the sitting room, where his mother was seated with an older man in tinted lenses. Angelica's back was to the door.

"James, where have you been?" Angelica snapped. "Dinner was on the table twenty—" Her voice died in her throat as she turned to face him. "My God," she whispered.

James could feel the blood gushing from the wound on his face. He nodded at his mother, who stood and turned away. James tried not to feel hurt. He and his mother had a **tacit** understanding—she couldn't stand the sight of blood, especially James's blood. She had never been able to take care of him when he was bleeding.

respiration: breathing
eclectic: varied or quirky
idiosyncratic: peculiar to an individual
elegant: stylish or tasteful
tacit: unspoken or implied

"Alistair," Angelica said to the older gentleman seated on the chaise, "would you—"

"Of course," Alistair said smoothly, as though he knew all about Angelica's aversion to blood, eager to help. "Why don't you go upstairs?" His voice held the traces of a **dialect** that James couldn't place.

"James, this is Alistair Masterson," Angelica said.

"Pleased to meet you," James gasped, remembering to speak formally, the way his mother liked.

Alistair smiled. "The pleasure is all mine, I can assure you."

Angelica nodded. She didn't look at James as she wobbled from the room. "Alistair," she said as she paused in the doorway, "don't forget who—and what—you're dealing with." Then she hurried up the stairs.

James frowned at his mother's **cryptic** words. What was that about? He was used to his mum acting a little melodramatic about stuff, but since when was he a "what" to deal with? He tried to bury the feelings of resentment that bubbled to the surface, threatening to break through, as he sank onto an overstuffed wing chair. His mother's sudden departure had made his day reach its **nadir**. *Don't think about it,* he commanded himself, but of course it was pointless. He couldn't push away the thought that any other mother would have stayed to take care of her injured son or would have at least asked what happened. But hadn't he learned by now that his mother was anything but the typical mum?

"Would you like to tell me how this happened?" Alistair asked as he stood up from his chair. He was very tall, and his figure was trim and fashionable in a well-cut black suit with a Nehru collar. *Armani?* James wondered. Whoever the designer, James was certain the suit had cost roughly the same amount of money that his semester's tuition had.

"It happened about how you would think it happened," James re-

dialect: regional language **cryptic:** mysterious or puzzling **nadir:** low point

plied. "I was robbed."

Alistair bent and inspected James's injuries with an impassive eye. "Perhaps we should call a doctor," the old gentleman suggested.

James cringed. "It's not as bad as it looks," he said. "Besides, the blood has already begun to **coagulate**, and if the doctor reopens the wounds, there's a higher risk of infection." This made no sense and wasn't even true, and James wasn't sure why he said it. All he knew was that he didn't want a doctor showing up there, not if he could avoid it.

Alistair smiled, seeming to understood James's attempt at **obfuscation**. Even though he was sure that it wasn't meant to be **patronizing**, James felt a spike of irritation, anyway.

"I should be able to take care of this myself," James said bitterly. "I'm in my last year of medical school." His arms dangled weakly by his sides.

"But you know that wouldn't be **judicious**." Alistair's voice was soothing and deep . . . and James found it familiar somehow. "Do you have a first-aid kit?"

"Under the sink," James replied, "in the kitchen."

Alistair disappeared for a moment and then returned with the orange plastic first aid kit. His mother had never kept one in the house when he was young, but when James had started medical school and had heard that most injuries occurred in the home, he had insisted they get one. James **flinched** as the old gentleman cleaned his wounds and staunched the bleeding on his cheekbone. He found Melinda, the housekeeper, and asked for some ice and fresh clothes. James winced as the ice was raised to his swollen eyes, but after a moment he got **acclimated** to the cold and began to feel better. Alistair's touch was light and gentle, and he clearly knew what he was doing, which made the fact that a stranger was treating his wounds a little easier to take.

coagulate: clot
obfuscation: concealment
patronizing: condescending or belittling
judicious: wise
flinched: cringed
acclimated: adjusted or accustomed

Alistair **meticulously** cleaned up every trace of blood and sent Melinda to find James a new set of clothes. He even excused himself while James changed into the clean, soft white shirt and khaki pants.

"Drink this," Alistair said as he walked back into the room, carrying a snifter. In it was a gleaming liquid of a dark amber color.

Brandy. James's mother was always giving him the stuff, which still felt weird even after James was technically old enough to drink it. His friends' parents sure didn't keep brandy around for their kids. But right now James didn't care. He downed the drink quickly, grimacing as it burned his throat. But it did make him feel better.

"I've sent the girl to fetch Angelica," Alistair said in his quiet voice.

James reached for the ice pack and held it against his eye as he leaned back on the sofa. "How do you know my mother, anyway?" James asked.

"We're old friends," Alistair replied.

"That's weird—I've never heard of you." James let an edge of suspicion creep into his voice. He liked this man, but there was something strange about him—something that James couldn't put his finger on.

But Alistair didn't take the bait. "Yes," he agreed, "it is strange."

Just then Melinda walked shyly into the room and handed Alistair a message. She was in her mid-thirties and had worked for Angelica for five years. In that time James had never heard her utter more than twenty words. She always just crept noiselessly around the house, cooking and cleaning, wearing her unobtrusive and self-imposed uniform of a black T-shirt and dark jeans. But now she seemed fascinated by Alistair. James noticed that she couldn't keep her eyes off him as he scanned the message. Alistair didn't pay any mind to the attention, though, and when he finished, he merely gave Melinda a nod of dismissal. "It seems that your mother isn't

meticulously: carefully or thoroughly

feeling well," Alistair announced as he stood and brushed off his elegant jacket. "We'll have to have our little dinner party another night. Which is just as well . . . you need your rest." He gave James a slight bow. "I hope to see you again soon," he said in a courtly manner.

"Yes, so do I," James agreed. He struggled to stand, but Alistair waved at him dismissively.

"I'll show myself out," Alistair said quickly. "Please, rest." With that, Alistair swept from the room in the same dramatic way James's mum always did.

James watched him go. Part of him did hope to see the old man again. But part of him doubted that would ever happen.

After all, his mother never seemed to have the same man over twice.

* * * * *

James woke up, every muscle in his body screaming in pain. For a moment he was confused . . . and then the previous night's **debacle** came flooding back. **Rancor** pulsed through his veins as every insignificant detail flashed through his mind . . . the way the first man **abducted** him, dragging him into the alley, James's **hapless** attempts to fight off his attackers, the **malevolent** faces of the men, James's own **ignominious** failure to stop the crime. He glanced at the glowing numbers on the digital clock—11 A.M. What day was it? James had to rack his brain to remember. Thursday? He glanced at the calendar above his desk to **validate** his guess. No, Friday. James shot up in bed, realizing he was already late to class. But the sudden move sent ripples of pain through his body. *Fine,* James thought, *whether or not to go to class is hardly a* ***quandary****. I can miss one day.* Ms. Finn's **epidemiology** class was pretty **vapid**, anyway. Ms. Finn usually only chose the **salient** points from the textbook

debacle: incident or misfortune
rancor: bitterness or resentment
abducted: kidnapped
hapless: unlucky or unsuccessful
malevolent: wicked
ignominious: humiliating
validate: confirm
quandary: dilemma
epidemiology: study of the presence or absence of diseases
vapid: dull
salient: most important

and made them over and over in an endless **harangue** that lasted an hour longer than it needed to. James could just do the reading and cover the material himself. Missing class was no **calamity**. He needed to rest. But more than rest, he needed something to eat. He hadn't eaten since lunch the day before, and he was famished. Besides, he thought, some food might **quell** the pain that still tore through his body.

James lurched out of bed and threw on some clothes, pausing to look in the mirror. The **palette** of his face had changed—instead of pinks and flesh tones, his skin was disfigured with blues and purples and the deep red cut that licked across his cheekbone. James muttered a **malediction** at the men who did this to him, then wobbled downstairs to the kitchen.

Angelica was already sitting at the breakfast table, poring over the newspaper with a cup of coffee in her hand. She hated computers and refused to get her news online.

"French toast?" she asked without looking up from her paper.

James stared at her. Her ability to guess what he wanted to eat at any given moment was **uncanny**. She could also usually predict what he was going to do. James had heard his friends complain about the way their parents seemed to have eyes in the back of their heads, but with Angelica, it was more. It was almost as though she could see directly into his mind. It gave him the creeps sometimes.

"Yes, French toast," James murmured as he slipped into a chair.

Angelica stood up and walked to the stove. She was still wearing her dressing gown, but she had tied an apron over it. The **juxtaposition** of his glamorous mother with her long dark hair and satin dressing gown fussing with an apron struck James as funny, but it would have hurt to laugh.

James watched his mother crack the eggs into a bowl and add milk. He was nearly hypnotized by the **unctuous** mixture as Angelica whipped it quickly in the glass bowl.

harangue: lecture or rant
calamity: disaster
quell: subdue or suppress
palette: set of colors
malediction: curse
uncanny: eerie
juxtaposition: side-by-side comparison
unctuous: fatty, oily

"Juice?" Angelica asked, snapping him out of his reverie.

James didn't want the juice, but he also knew that his mother would cajole him into having it, so he just nodded and accepted the glass she offered him. James noticed that his mother's dark eyes stayed trained on the floor while she handed him the glass. She still couldn't look at his face. "You should take some aspirin," Angelica murmured. She turned back to the counter and dipped a piece of bread into the egg and milk, then set it hissing into the pan.

James knew that aspirin might **palliate** his pain, but for some reason, he didn't want to take it. Instead he changed the subject. "What are you doing up so early?"

"Isn't a mother allowed to make breakfast for her son?" Angelica answered **obliquely.** She handed James the plate of French toast, then pulled a bottle of maple syrup from the cupboard. It was imported from Canada, and James loved the stuff.

James shook his head. If his mother didn't want to explain why she was awake before noon, he wouldn't make her. The fact was, Angelica rarely ever rose before lunch and even then usually kept the shades drawn during the day. She was sensitive to light, she said. All of the bulbs in the house were soft pink incandescent lights. Angelica swore that she would never have a halogen lamp anywhere in her house. And Angelica never went outside until after dark, when she attended endless rounds of charity events. She didn't have a real job—she didn't have to. When James's father died almost nineteen years ago, he had left behind a sizable fortune, including the town house they lived in and a trust fund for James. So Angelica was a professional socialite, an occupation that kept her mostly amused and worked with the hours she preferred.

James gobbled up his French toast with a **ravenous** abandon that surprised him. His mother watched him attack his food with a **bemused** smile.

"I can always make more," Angelica said gently.

palliate: relieve
obliquely: indirectly

ravenous: starving or greedy

bemused: puzzled or absentminded

James looked up and caught her eye for a moment, and then she looked away.

"I can't stand what they've done to you," she said. Her face had turned white again, this time with anger. "I can't believe this happened so close to our house." Her fist slammed down on the table, rattling her coffee cup in its saucer.

James placed a hand over her fist. "It's all right," he said gently. "I'm fine." But deep down, he was happy that she finally seemed upset about what had happened. As strange as she was, she was still his mum, and he felt better seeing that she really did care about him. He looked at her beautiful, delicate face. James had seen his mother's wedding photographs, and she didn't seem to have aged a single day in the twenty-three years that had passed. Her skin was still perfectly smooth and bone white, like china. Her green eyes sparkled with a familiar intensity, and her hair hung in long, **lush** waves. When they were seen together, many people mistook Angelica for James's sister. Now there were worried creases at the corners of her eyes, and it made her seem more motherly. But the feeling lasted only a moment. Then Angelica stood up and took her coffee cup to the sink.

"Soon you won't have to worry about this kind of thing anymore," she murmured.

James frowned, wondering what she meant. He hadn't come right out and told her yet about his plan to go away after he got his medical degree, but he'd been dropping some hints, hoping to warm her up to the idea. Maybe she'd figured out more than he'd realized, in that way she had.

"Alistair is coming to dinner tomorrow night," Angelica said as James brought his empty plate to the sink. "I was hoping that you would join us."

"Sure," James replied. Then, impulsively, he gave her a kiss on the cheek and walked out of the kitchen. So he would see Alistair

lush: luxuriant

again after all. His assumptions about his mother had been **fallacious.** He was glad he'd been wrong. There was something about Alistair's **sagacity** that had struck James. In their single interaction, he felt they'd built something of a **rapport.** Besides, James wanted to thank Alistair for everything he had done for him. And he was curious to know more about his connection to James's mum. Why did the old man seem so familiar?

There was no question that tomorrow would be a very interesting evening.

fallacious: incorrect

sagacity: air of wisdom

rapport: personal connection

Chapter Two

A **zephyr** blew across his face, he shut his eyes, feeling the breeze against his skin. A cold front had moved in that morning, bringing the first frosty air of winter. James loved the crisp solitude of late fall—the way the trees of Hyde Park turned red and golden and the promise of breathtaking fireworks for Guy Fawkes Night. It was his favorite time of year.

Suddenly there was a **cacophony** of voices below, and the solemn **knell** of the door chime. James wished people would just use the knocker—his mother had chosen a doorbell with a chime that seemed almost absurd in its **gravity,** something you'd find in a church instead of a private home. But Angelica insisted she liked it, completely **oblivious** to its funereal sound.

James hurried downstairs. Angelica had already led Alistair into the drawing room, and James greeted him **genially.** Suddenly, James saw that Alistair had brought a younger man with him.

"This is Francis Milton," Alistair said.

"It's nice to meet you," James said, holding out his hand.

Francis looked at James with cold gray eyes and hesitated a moment before accepting James's handshake. "It's a pleasure," he said without warmth. His hand was cool and smooth, but there was something **nefarious** in his glance that sent a shudder through James. The feeling was **nebulous,** but almost palpable in its force.

After a moment, Melinda came in to announce that dinner was on the table. All four followed her into the dining room, which had been laid out according to Angelica's specifications, with the best linen and silver in the house. The tall candlesticks gleamed between a large, fragrant bouquet of white roses and lilies, studded here and

zephyr: light wind
cacophony: harsh, discordant sound
knell: ring
gravity: seriousness
oblivious: unaware
genially: warmly or graciously
nefarious: evil
nebulous: vague

there with beaded dragonflies, giving the whole arrangement a **whimsical** touch. James was surprised at the light and airy décor. It was almost **ebullient**—like a fairy had decorated the room. His mother usually stuck with dark reds, blacks, and browns.

"So, James," Alistair said as Melinda placed a delicate portion of tenderloin on his plate, "I hear that you're the star of next year's graduating class at Wilcox." He gazed at James through his tinted lenses, and James flushed.

"Well, I have been given a teaching assistantship," he admitted, "and I did well on my exams last year."

"Don't let James fool you," Angelica said smoothly. "He's worked hard, and he's going to graduate at the top of his class."

"Yes, Alistair mentioned that you're planning on being a doctor," Francis said. A bemused smile played at the corners of his lips. "Why on earth would you want to do that?" He laughed, spearing a piece of squash with his fork. "There's not as much money in medicine as there used to be. The real opportunities are in business." Francis's words were **banal,** but his hard gray eyes held something that James thought was **tantamount** to a challenge.

"I want to help people," James said earnestly. "I kind of think people who have more should make an effort to even things out with everyone else."

Alistair smiled at James. "Charming," he said quietly.

"Yes, charming," Francis echoed, although his tone was mocking. "But isn't that argument a little **facile**? Not to mention old-fashioned?"

"Why's that?" James asked.

"Well, where does the doctor fit into the natural order of things?" Francis asked. "Why do we insist on prolonging life as much as possible—even for people who are really of no use to society—like the elderly or terminal invalids? Shouldn't those people be allowed to die? Isn't that what Darwin was saying? That only the

whimsical: unusual or fanciful
ebullient: bright and cheerful

banal: ordinary or predictable

tantamount: roughly the same as
facile: simplistic

strong survive? And that natural selection is what's best for the species in the long run?" Francis gave James a tight little smile and took a bite of steak.

James stared at him, taking in for the first time Francis's black turtleneck and wide-wale corduroy pants. Right. Francis was one of those Chelsea intellectuals—the snotty rich kids who played at being poor, pursued "artistic" careers and spent hours drinking coffee and arguing about the meaning of life. James knew the type—they hung out in the Bloomsbury cafés, smoking, doing nothing. He'd had plenty in his school.

Alistair had been listening closely to Francis's argument, and now he looked expectantly at James.

"Look, I'm not trying to make an **edict** that everyone has to help others," James protested. "It just happens to be what I want to do with *my* life. Besides," he went on, "under your argument, there would be no doctors at all, which would lead to the deaths of even healthy people. You can't **abdicate** your responsibility to everyone, right?"

"Why not?" Francis demanded. "**Laissez-faire** existence. Let people fend for themselves, as the cavemen did."

"Yes, and isn't it true that the world is overpopulated?" Alistair chimed in, leaning forward in his chair slightly. James noticed that he hadn't touched his food. "After all, when the deer population grows too large, people are encouraged to hunt them. Otherwise the deer would starve. Surely the same attitude—which is really an attitude of mercy—should be applied to all people? Perhaps our *dear* Francis has a point."

James wanted to reply, but he was distracted by Alistair's words. There was something about the way Alistair said "our dear Francis" that sounded in James's mind like "our *deer,* Francis." Was Alistair trying to say that Francis could be a victim of his own logic? James wasn't sure whether Alistair was on his side or not.

edict: law or decree

abdicate: abandon

laissez-faire: free of interference with freedom of choice

He looked at his mother, who'd kept quiet all this time, hoping that she would leap to his defense. But her mouth was closed tightly in a grim line.

"Well," James said uncomfortably, "I guess we'll just have to agree to disagree."

"I guess so," Francis said, leaning back in his chair in a triumphant pose.

"Very interesting," Alistair murmured, and turned to his food.

With one glance at him, James was certain that this had been some sort of test. And that he had failed.

* * * * *

James struggled through dinner somehow, paying particular attention to his food, eating **fastidiously,** wiping his lips after every bite, hoping to appear more like a **gourmand** and less like someone who didn't want to talk to his dinner guests. It wasn't that he had expected **kudos** for his views on helping people; it was just that he couldn't **fathom** the opposite view—that people should be allowed to suffer and die as some sort of social experiment. The worst part was that he was left feeling as though his own arguments had been **fatuous** and that he hadn't said what he had really meant at all. As he watched Francis pick at his vegetables, James was sure that the young man had purposely intended to **goad** him into a fight from the very start—that the whole argument had been perfectly **calibrated** to make James feel like an idiot. James just wished that he was more used to debating so that he could quickly **debunk** Francis's **callous** theories. But when it came to arguments, he was a **neophyte,** and it showed. He couldn't defend himself in a pillow fight, either.

He wished that Alistair and Francis would go home.

"Shall we?"

fastidiously: carefully or delicately
gourmand: food lover or connoisseur
kudos: praise
fathom: understand or grasp
fatuous: stupid or childish
goad: provoke
calibrated: adjusted or set up
debunk: expose as untrue
callous: heartless
neophyte: beginner

James looked over and saw his mother smiling at him.

"I'm sorry." James shook his head. "What did you say?"

"Your son has been **immersed** in his own thoughts throughout dinner," Alistair said with a small smile. "I suppose he's found our conversation rather **tedious.**"

"Not at all," Angelica said quickly, in a tone that was meant to **upbraid** James as well as to **salve** Alistair's hurt feelings. James somehow doubted whether Alistair was, in fact, hurt by the fact that James had been a **negligent** host. He was almost sure that Alistair had been teasing him . . . and maybe trying to tell him that he, too, found Francis boring. "James is often in his own world, lost in the **fecund** depths of his mind."

Angelica gave James a **winsome** smile, and he knew he'd better pay more attention to their guests. When his mother became annoyed or angry, she would always become overly polite to mask her sarcastic tone . . . which was what she was doing now.

"I'm sorry, Mum," James said politely, but not **obsequiously.** "What were you saying?"

"I was just suggesting that we retire to the sitting room," Angelica said smoothly, "for a nightcap."

More of that overly polite, superformal language—Angelica wasn't asking; she was giving him a **mandate.**

"Of course," James said **rashly.** The truth was, he didn't want to spend a second more with Francis. *I should have thought of a reason to leave,* James thought. He could have excused himself to go study or said that he was still tired from the attack the night before. But James had never been **wily.**

James chose a comfortable wing chair before the fire in the sitting room and sank into it. He stared at the fire, contemplating the **variegated** orange flames **undulating** like snakes as they licked the wood.

A silence descended over the guests. James looked over at his

immersed: absorbed
tedious: boring or tiresome
upbraid: scold
salve: soothe or heal
negligent: careless or inattentive
fecund: fertile
winsome: pleasant
obsequiously: in an overly flattering or polite manner
mandate: go-ahead or permission
rashly: hastily or without thinking
wily: clever or cunning
variegated: multicolored or flecked
undulating: moving in waving or rolling fashion

mother, feeling muddled by all the strange thoughts running through his head. She sat there, looking beautiful in her **diaphanous** top. The shirt was elaborately embroidered with butterflies, and she wore it with a pair of designer jeans. Angelica did all of her shopping over the phone—she had long-standing relationships with several Paris **couture** houses—and always managed to look about a thousand times hipper than her own son. James just wasn't into clothing—he'd grab a pair of khaki pants and an oxford shirt, and that was always fine for him. Alistair was standing near her, and Angelica's face was half **obscured** by the long shadow he cast as he stood before the fire. James felt like the shadow didn't belong there—it was almost like a malevolent being, bent on **effacing** his mother's features. He wanted to brush it away. And there was no doubt that his mother was unusually reserved tonight, her face more **pallid** than normal. Usually Angelica was **effervescent,** bubbling over with light conversation. But not tonight. James had never seen her this way before. He remembered that Alistair had said that he had known Angelica for a long time, and wondered what secret connection they shared.

"Perhaps some port?" Alistair suggested suddenly. He looked at Angelica, and his eyes held a certain **vehemence.**

"Yes," she said, and stood up deliberately, "it's time." James watched her carefully as she crossed to the decanter that was kept full on a nearby table. There was something odd about her—a determined tone in her voice, a certain **temerity** in her step—that put James on edge.

It's time—time for what? he wondered, shifting uncomfortably. This whole scene was getting way too weird.

Angelica poured the wine into four glasses. She handed one each to Alistair and Francis, then crossed the room to give one to James. James held the glass up before the fire, a mixture of pride and nervousness welling inside him. He had never been invited to

diaphanous: sheer or see-through
couture: high fashion
obscured: hidden
effacing: erasing or wiping out
pallid: pale
effervescent: lively or bubbly
vehemence: intensity
temerity: boldness or brashness

drink his mother's special port before. He drank other things, but never this. Why was she giving it to him now, on top of all the other bizarre things going on? James swirled the glass, and the liquid ran thickly around the rim, giving off a sweet **scent** that thoroughly **debauched** him.

He took a small sip, savoring the sweet wine, which seemed to affect his senses immediately. "Wow—this stuff is really strong," he thought suddenly. James's movements felt leaden, his mind sluggish, as though it was encased in something **viscous.** James looked around and saw both his mother and Alistair staring at him. But while Angelica's gaze was intense, Alistair's was impassive, his **immutable** eyes revealing none of his thoughts. James's mind reeled. Why did his mother's skin seem so pale? Why were her eyes so cold and brilliant, glittering with a strange, unnatural fierceness? Suddenly Angelica's beauty seemed like an **aberration.** Alistair, too, seemed impossibly handsome, his skin smoother and more perfect than any human skin, his eyes dark and dangerous.

Alistair smiled at James, revealing long, sharp canine teeth.

James blinked, feeling his heart race. Wait—that couldn't have been real. Was this a hallucination or something? The **laceration** on his cheekbone began to pulse with fresh pain.

Angelica sat down next to James. Her skin was almost translucent now, as if it were **illuminated** by a fire within. She had never looked so beautiful . . . or so terrifying.

James gulped, looking down at the glass in his hand. His thoughts went to the lessons he'd had in school on mind-altering substances, and he felt a jolt of fear. "What did you give me?" he whispered, his stomach clenching.

"A **panacea,**" Angelica said, leaning toward him. "It can cure anything."

Angelica gave James a gentle kiss on the cheek, then moved her lips to his neck. James moved to push her away, but he was too

scent: odor
debauched: seduced, corrupted
viscous: thick or gooey
immutable: unchanging
aberration: something that is odd or abnormal
laceration: rough cut or tear
illuminated: lit
panacea: a universal cure or remedy

slow. Pain shot through his neck as his mother bit down. James tried to cry out but couldn't force out anything more than a strangled gasp. He felt his body growing weaker, and his vision grew dim. His senses were shutting down—noises were coming to him as though from a great distance, and he knew that he was about to black out.

Angelica pulled back, and James could see that her lips were red, wet with his own blood. His eyes widened in horror. He'd always known his mother was different, strange. But this was too much—it was crazy, insane, like James was having some terrible nightmare. Was that it? Was he still sleeping? James tried to jerk his head to wake himself, but he knew somehow that he was absolutely, one hundred percent awake.

His mother pressed her index finger against her bottom lip, lifting a drop of blood. Then she held her finger out toward James, who **recoiled** instantly. But he was too weak to get away or even to resist as Angelica held his lips open and let the blood drop from her finger into his mouth. The coppery, salty taste of blood filled his senses, overpowering him. Suddenly James was overcome with desire—desire for this blood. He had to have more. His need filled him with a newfound strength, and without thinking, he leaned toward his mother and sank his own teeth into her neck.

Angelica didn't struggle as he drained her; in fact, she just stroked his hair. "Drink," she whispered. "Drink deeply."

James hardly heard her—he was too **immersed** in what he was doing. He couldn't stop. His senses were coming back. Colors leapt at James, muddling his vision in a **raucous** dance. Angelica lifted her arm, and the rustle of fabric it produced seemed to James like a searing symphony. He felt powerful, strong. A quick image of the thugs who robbed him flashed through his mind, and James was suddenly certain that he could crush them if he had to face them now. He could kill them without even trying. . . .

recoiled: shrank away

immersed: absorbed, focused

raucous: wild or rowdy

Angelica shoved him away, sending James gasping and reeling against the edge of the couch. James lunged toward her again, but Alistair placed an iron hand on James's arm.

"No more," Alistair murmured. "You'll kill her."

James shook his head, trying to clear it. He felt like he was underwater. His body was strong, but his mind was **murky.** Alistair grinned at him again with a glance of cold satisfaction. James's stomach tightened again at the sight of those impossible teeth.

Suddenly Alistair turned and looked behind him, where Francis was **cowering** in a corner. James had completely forgotten he was there.

"Please," Francis begged. His eyes were huge—he looked terrified. He had watched the whole thing.

"Please what?" Alistair's voice was a low growl as he stepped toward the young man.

"Have mercy," Francis begged. His voice was a whisper.

"Mercy?" Alistair repeated, laughing cruelly. "By your own argument, Francis, mercy is a useless emotion. Why shouldn't the strong prey on the weak?"

Angelica stood up and moved toward Francis. Francis tried to bolt, but Angelica seized his arm and dragged him backward. Through the haze of his mind James felt himself trying to scream, to stop her and Alistair from hurting Francis. This was wrong—everything that was happening here was very wrong, and James wished with every fiber of his being that he could make it all stop. But he couldn't make a sound or move from his spot.

Alistair ran his hand tenderly through Francis's hair, then yanked down, hard, exposing his neck. Francis didn't have time to let out a cry before Angelica and Alistair sank their teeth into the white flesh of his throat.

James watched all of this in horror, but then his senses overwhelmed him and the room went black.

murky: dark or muddy

cowering: crouching or trembling

* * * * *

James opened his eyes groggily, feeling like he'd been hit by a train. Every inch of his body throbbed in silent protest to the most **minuscule** movement. Right, he'd been beaten up by those thugs. How long had he been sleeping?

No, wait. James squeezed his eyes shut as the horrible events of the night before burned through his mind like a bolt of lightning. Every detail of Francis's death came back with horrifying clarity—his pallid skin, the look of fear that had contorted his features. That—that couldn't have happened . . . could it? Could his mother and Alistair really have . . . ? No. No, it wasn't possible. It was a dream, like he'd thought. Francis was fine. Suddenly James didn't mind the pain. He was just glad that he had finally woken up from the **harrowing** nightmare that had plagued his sleep.

James struggled to sit up and rubbed his face. He had a horrible headache—the pain was so intense that he had to squint as he looked around him. It took him a moment to realize that he was not in his own room.

This room, unlike his, resembled the rest of his mother's house, decorated in dark colors with formal furniture. The bed was a four-poster, made of richly carved wood. The rug on the floor was an expensive Oriental carpet, **lavishly** woven with brilliant colors. The sheets were soft as silk, made of pure Egyptian cotton. For a moment James had the unearthly sensation that he wasn't himself—that he had somehow slipped into someone else's life. Where were his posters of David Beckham and Manchester United, his familiar textbooks, his stereo and CDs?

He hauled himself out of bed and crossed to a mahogany dresser, staring into the gilt-edged mirror above it. Swallowing back his growing fear, he looked at his reflection, then gasped. The man in the mirror was both him and not him. It was the same familiar face,

minuscule: tiny

harrowing: stressful or worrying

lavishly: richly or extravagantly

but his eyes . . . They glittered with a strange ferocity, and they seemed to glow with a new shade of green. His skin, too, seemed to glow. And his wounds . . . they were completely healed.

"Amazing, isn't it?" said a voice behind him.

James whirled to see a girl around his age standing in the doorway. Long auburn hair hung halfway down her back, and she was wearing urban camouflage pants and a tight spandex top. She was also wearing sunglasses, even in the dimly lit room.

"Do you always wear those indoors?" James blurted.

She ignored his question. "I'm Susan," she said.

"Okay, Susan," James said as he folded his arms across his chest, "would you mind telling me where the hell I am?"

Susan smiled softly. "You're at Alistair Masterson's estate. We're a few miles outside of London."

"What am I doing here?"

Susan shrugged. "Your family must have sent you here. Alistair is a tutor—"

"Good morning," Alistair said as he strode into the room. He was wearing a long black **duster** and his usual tinted glasses. "Susan," he said brightly, "perhaps you could go see what Adam is doing in the kitchen. I'm afraid we'll never have breakfast at this rate."

Susan nodded and left.

"Would you mind explaining what the bloody hell's going on?" James demanded.

Alistair smiled faintly and crossed the room to the window. James had to fight a rising feeling of panic. Somehow he hadn't noticed the bars on the exterior.

"Your mother felt it would be in your best interest to come here," Alistair said. "You are here with her full permission. She thought it would be best after the Change."

"Change?" James repeated as a cold snake of dread slithered down his spine. "What change? What are you talking about?"

duster: a long coat

Alistair turned and leered at James. "You know," he said simply.

"I don't," James protested feebly. His mind was swimming. *I'll get an attorney,* he thought hazily. *They can't keep me here. I'm not a minor. This is kidnapping.*

"My dear James," Alistair said smoothly, "you have become one of us now, a vampire, of course."

Chapter Three

"You're insane," James whispered. *I can't be a vampire,* he thought, his mind reeling. *It's* ***untenable.*** *Vampires don't exist.*

"Really, James, I'm disappointed in you," Alistair replied. He frowned, and his glance held a **rebuke.**

"It can't be true," James repeated, hoping to pierce the older gentleman's **veneer.** His mind clung **obstinately** to the idea that this was nothing but a pack of lies, that if only he could debunk Alistair's logic, this whole conversation would end. "I can see myself in the mirror!"

Alistair laughed. "Of course you can," he said. "You have a body, don't you? Vampires have many powers. We can make ourselves very difficult so see, but we can't make ourselves invisible."

"Vampires don't exist."

"Oh, really?" Alistair drew himself up **haughtily,** then lunged at James's hand and grasped his wrist. He traced his finger along the inside of James's wrist **languidly.** James noticed that although Alistair's face was handsome in the way of a man in his late fifties or early sixties, his hand seemed much older—**wizened** and almost clawlike.

"Do you mind?" Alistair asked **felicitously.** He blinked at James **benignly.**

James was too frightened to reply. He wasn't sure what the older gentleman was asking, and he didn't dare say either yes or no.

In the next moment Alistair lashed out with a movement that was almost too quick for James to see. James cried out as Alistair slashed open his wrist.

James stared up at Alistair, who returned his look with a **san-**

untenable: invalid or incorrect
rebuke: scolding or reprimand
veneer: mask or guise
obstinately: stubbornly
haughtily: proudly
languidly: slowly or lazily
wizened: wrinkled or aged
felicitously: pleasantly
benignly: kindly or harmlessly
sanguine: cheerful

guine smile. James screamed in pain and clamped his hand to his wrist. Blood oozed between his fingers.

"Let go," Alistair commanded.

James didn't remove his hand—he had to staunch the bleeding. Alistair reached out and ripped James's hand from his wrist.

When James looked down at his wrist, he saw that the delicate bones and veins of his arm lay **manifest** before his eyes. *What's happening?* James wondered, his mind struggling to **comprehend** the **paradox.** He was cut, but the flesh seemed to be knitting together.

"A vampire won't bleed unless he has fed recently."

James's mind lurched, searching among his **manifold** lessons in hematology for a reason that this could be happening. But he couldn't think of a single one. His hopes were **razed** in a single blow. James backed away from Alistair, whose previously **venerable** demeanor suddenly seemed threatening. "What have you done to me?"

"What have I done to you?" Alistair repeated. "Don't you understand that you're standing at the door to **utopia**? Your life has become a new **paradigm,** one that you could never have begun to imagine only hours ago."

"You're insane—this is disgusting," James snarled. "I don't want anything to do with this, any of it." His wrist was now perfectly healed, with no sign that it had ever been injured.

"Enough with this false **sanctimoniousness**," Alistair said. James had noticed that when Alistair was **frustrated,** his usual **laconic** speech descended into **grandiloquence.** "Don't give yourself **grandiose** notions of victimhood," Alistair went on. "You are a vampire because you did it to yourself. Your mother offered you the blood, and you drank it."

"No—" James protested.

"I can tolerate many things," Alistair spat, "but self-deception is something I cannot **abide.** I **abhor** it as much as I do a liar. *You* did

manifest: visible or apparent
comprehend: understand
paradox: impossibility
manifold: numerous or various
razed: destroyed
venerable: dignified
utopia: ideal world
paradigm: example or model
sanctimoniousness: false respect
frustrated: annoyed or thwarted
laconic: short or to the point
grandiloquence: showy wordiness
grandiose: self-important or showy
abide: put up with
abhor: hate

this." He pointed at James and stepped closer so that their faces were only inches apart. James could see Alistair's perfect skin, the tiny pores invisible. "You *chose* it."

James stumbled backward, but he knew that no matter how much he wanted these words to be **calumny,** they weren't. It was the truth. Images from the night before flooded his mind as he recalled the **hedonistic** abandon with which he had let himself feed. The memory was **repugnant** to him, yet . . . yet James recalled it with **lurid** fascination.

He raised his eyes to meet Alistair's.

"Don't you feel the difference in yourself?" Alistair asked. He walked to the window and flung the curtains wide. "You're dead, and you'll never have to die again. Take a look outside."

James took a **tentative** step toward the window, then crossed the room quickly. It was dark, and James wondered how long he had been asleep. But that thought flew quickly from his mind as he realized that his vision had changed—it was like a cat's, perfectly suited to the night. He could see everything—birds nestled in nests on tree limbs, squirrels and chipmunks darting here and there. Every leaf on the tall boxwood hedge at the edge of the garden seemed to shimmer slightly, glowing dimly in the darkness. He could see perfectly, as though his eyes had infrared sensors. The scene that lay before him was suffused with light.

"You have become a **nocturnal** creature," Alistair explained, placing his hand on James's shoulder. "And now you see like one."

James looked at Alistair as closely as he could while still remaining **decorous.** There was something about the older man's tone—it seemed almost **wistful.** But in the next moment Alistair switched back to his usual businesslike style.

"Vampires have excellent vision—we can see the life light in things," Alistair went on. "But normal light can be . . . disturbing. That's why so many of us choose to wear sunglasses or tinted lenses

calumny: lies
hedonistic: wild or pleasure-seeking
repugnant: disgusting
lurid: shocking or vivid
tentative: cautious or hesitant
nocturnal: active at night
decorous: proper or polite
wistful: thoughtful or sad

even at night."

"Then all of those stories about how vampires won't go into the sun—" James began.

"Perfectly true," Alistair cut him off. "The brilliance of the sun is the **bane** of a vampire's existence. Even a few seconds of sunlight can be blinding. And it's the sun's heat can sear our skin. . . . More than a few moments of exposure is **excruciating.** But even these dim lamps can bother some vampires," Alistair finished, nodding at the lamp beside the bed. "You may want to take advantage of the sunglasses we've put at your bedside. You'll find there's no **dearth** of tinted lenses in the house—we've placed sunglasses in every room in case you misplace a pair and need one immediately."

James put on the sunglasses and found that his headache disappeared almost instantly.

Alistair smiled at him, and James felt an odd sense of **camaraderie** with this older man. "Would you care to see the mansion?" Alistair asked.

James nodded. Suddenly, he wanted to see everything.

*   *   *   *   *

". . . and this is the library," Alistair said as he pulled open the door to a large room lined with bookshelves.

James stepped inside and breathed in the smell of old leather. He pulled a book from the shelf entitled *Occult Wonders from Around the World.*

"There is fiction as well," Alistair said, "but we do have a **battery** of volumes on vampires and the occult in general. Very useful stuff, in case you want to do some research."

James's glance fell on a collection of knives and axes that hung on the wall. At the top was a long, slim sword, beautiful in its sparse elegance.

bane: curse or great annoyance

excruciating: extremely painful

dearth: shortage or lack

camaraderie: friendship or brotherhood

battery: set or series

"My antique weapon collection," Alistair said as James crossed to get a closer look.

"They're incredible," James whispered as he glanced at the ancient **artifacts.**

"I've been collecting them for years," Alistair offered as he walked over to the wall and fingered a ceremonial dagger delicately. "Three hundred years," he added softly.

"The dagger is three hundred years old?" James asked, looking at it closely.

Alistair cocked an eyebrow at him. "The dagger is *seven* hundred years old," he clarified. "I have *collected* these for three hundred years."

James gaped at him. "How old are you?"

Alistair chuckled. "I am three hundred fifty years old. Don't be so surprised. There are many who are older than I am."

"And now you teach other vampires . . ."

"How to use their powers, yes," Alistair said. James glanced at the blade, then looked back at Alistair, but the older gentleman had disappeared. James whipped around. Where had Alistair gone? James looked around the library but couldn't see anything.

"Hello?" James called.

Just then Alistair stepped from the shadows of the far corner. James was amazed. His eyes had actually passed over Alistair as he looked around the room. Alistair had moved so silently and so quickly that James's eyes hadn't detected the movement.

"Amazing," James murmured.

"There's more," Alistair said urgently. "Much more. And I will teach you everything."

James nodded, suddenly overwhelmed by Alistair's presence. Still, Francis's death flashed in James's mind, and he was wary.

"But first I must tell you a few of the facts," Alistair said as he motioned James over to a couch. "There's so much fiction, and er-

artifacts: objects or relics

roneous information is dangerous."

"Wait—" James said, hoping that the older vampire wouldn't take his **query** as **effrontery.** "I have a question. The bed I slept in . . ."

"You don't have to sleep in a coffin," Alistair affirmed. "Why on earth would you need to sleep in a box when a perfectly dark room will suffice? Just be sure that the curtains are drawn. And yes," Alistair went on, anticipating James's next question, "you do need to feed on blood, but not every night. Vampires only need to feed once in every lunar phase, although they can choose to drink more. And many do."

"Does the blood have to be . . ." James could hardly bring himself to add, "Human?"

Alistair hesitated a moment, then shook his head. "It doesn't have to be," he said. "But I'm sure that you'll find you prefer human blood to any other kind."

James felt the immediate need to **repudiate** this statement. "I'm sure that won't be true in my case," he said quickly.

Alistair shrugged. "Now, listen closely," he said. "No matter what you feed on, it is vital that you drain the subject fully, until he or she is dead. Do you understand? Otherwise if that person should live and taste blood, they themselves will become a vampire."

James nodded, pouring every ounce of energy into absorbing what Alistair was telling him.

"Vampires need to be chosen carefully," Alistair went on. "The wrong kind of vampire could be dangerous not only to humans but also other vampires."

"You said before that we were immortal," James began.

"And so we are," Alistair affirmed, "although our powers are **finite.** We can be killed."

"A stake through the heart?" James asked.

"Yes, but only if it is delivered at the end of the lunar cycle, when

query: question

effrontery: rudeness or disrespect

repudiate: deny

finite: limited

a vampire hasn't fed," Alistair said. "Vampire power drains over time. Vampires are strong—**immeasurably** strong—when they have just fed. But after a few days without blood, a vampire is **vulnerable.** And if you go without feeding on the last day of the cycle, you will find yourself too weak to feed—and you will die of starvation. A hideous way to die, I can assure you." He adjusted his position on the couch. "Vampires can also be killed with fire, but not with water."

"Why not water?" James asked.

Alistair lifted his eyebrows at James, and that was when James realized that he hadn't been breathing. The normal rhythm of his breath was absent.

"Nor can vampires be harmed with crosses," Alistair went on. "There's nothing particularly mystical about us. We can be hurt with physical things—but not with an idea."

"What about garlic?" James asked.

Alistair grimaced. "**Noisome** stuff," he said, "but tolerable. The problem is that vampires, like all **predators,** have a strong sense of smell. So most strong odors are unwelcome, that's all. But since you don't *have* to breathe . . ."

"That girl who came up to my room," James asked, "is she a vampire, too?"

"Susan? Of course."

Suddenly James was overwhelmed by a realization he had carefully been keeping at bay, out of his consciousness. He sank down into the chair beside him, swallowing hard to keep from **regurgitating.**

"My—my mother . . ."

"Yes," Alistair confirmed. "Your mother is also a vampire, obviously."

Once again the image of his mother descending on Francis flashed through his mind, and it made him physically ill. It was

immeasurably: hugely or infinitely

vulnerable: weak or defenseless

noisome: harmful or nasty

predators: creatures that prey or feed on others

regurgitating: throwing up

true—he knew it was true. And really, it explained everything—all the strange things he'd always tried so hard not to wonder about. Why she only left the house at night, why she couldn't stand the sight of her son's blood, even why she never had the same man over twice . . . All of her eccentricities suddenly snapped into place. It even explained why she hated computers—the light from the screen probably bothered her eyes.

James looked around, wondering whether Angelica had been Alistair's student. They certainly seemed to know each other. Had he had taught her in this very room?

James didn't want to know the answer.

* * * * *

"We have over fifty acres here," Alistair said as he led James down a path behind the manor. The grounds were as **meticulously** cared for as the interior of the mansion and equally grand and beautiful, even by night. James's new, heightened senses allowed him to take in the grounds as a single, **organic** whole. The pristine lawns, the trim hedges, the towering oaks, everything shimmered in the darkness with its own life light.

"There is a lake behind the woods," Alistair said, gesturing to a cluster of oak trees. "It's a pleasant place to walk—you'll often find me there. And here," he added, leading James into a long, low building, "is the garage. You are welcome to use any of the vehicles. . . ." Alistair nodded to a line of beautiful cars. James had always been interested in automotive technology, and he was amazed to see the collection of vintage autos—the 1966 Shelby Mustang, the 1953 Corvette, the 1954 Gullwing Mercedes. James ran his hand along the Mercedes's glossy exterior. He peered in the window at the interior and once again nearly had to catch his breath at the sight of himself reflected in the glass.

meticulously: taking extreme care over details

organic: natural or living

"If you're interested in cars," Alistair went on, "you might want to talk to Adam here."

James looked up to see that a guy who looked a little younger than he—not that it meant much about his true age, James realized—had appeared behind Alistair. His features were fine and **angular,** and his glance was almost wolflike in its intensity. Adam's body was muscular, outlined by his tight T-shirt and brown leather pants, but his movements held a **subtle** and unexpected grace. He leaned **nonchalantly** against the gullwing and gave James a **beguiling,** lopsided grin. Adam held a helmet in the crook of his elbow, and in one fluid movement he hurled the helmet at James, who caught it easily.

"Do you ride?" Adam asked in a cocky tone.

James struggled to hide his annoyance. Adam obviously thought he was some kind of **maverick.** But he was probably just as dependent on Alistair as James was, and James didn't want Adam to think that he was superior just because he had been at the manor longer. James chucked the helmet back at Adam, putting some force behind the toss, then gave a **recalcitrant** shrug. "I've been on a motorbike," James said.

"Very good," Alistair said smoothly, stepping between the young men. "Perhaps, Adam, you wouldn't mind taking James along on your **quotidian** sojourn into the city?"

Adam smiled again, but the look in his eyes was **scathing.** His **animosity** toward James was more than evident. "If James can keep up, I don't care," Adam said. Then he turned on his heel and walked through a door at the other end of the garage.

James followed him and was surprised to step into another long, low room filled with a line of motorcycles. "Take your pick," Adam called over his shoulder as he walked toward a bike and straddled it.

A slim figure in a helmet and black leather pants was already astride a bike before the open garage door. Long auburn hair that

angular: lean or bony
subtle: faint or barely noticeable
nonchalantly: casually or coolly
beguiling: charming or enchanting
maverick: rebel
recalcitrant: defiant, resisting authority
quotidian: daily
scathing: searing
animosity: hostility or ill will

spilled from beneath the helmet told James it was Susan. She revved her engine at the sight of Adam, then turned and sped out the door. Adam kicked his starter and zoomed after her.

James wanted to linger over the beautiful machines, to **venerate** their **utilitarian** beauty, but he didn't want to be left behind. On impulse, he decided to take the Harley-Davidson, a **behemoth** with a powerful engine. James turned the key in the ignition and gave the starter a single, **tenuous** kick, and the machine started right up. In a moment he was speeding down the driveway, following the roar of the other two engines.

It didn't take long to catch up to the other two riders, and the three tore through the countryside in a single line. The moon hung like a jewel above them while the breeze blew cool against James's skin. Even through the dark visor of the helmet, the life lights glowed around him—the cows in their pastures, the small animals and—most brilliantly of all—the humans in their cars. They all had the aura of life—they were pulsing with light. James felt like he could **subsist** on the energy surrounding him alone, it was so powerful.

Smells, too, came fast and furious. At one moment it would be the sweet scent of clover in a field, at another the **fetid** odor of manure. A skunk, the oil on the pavement, feverfew crushed beneath a horse's hoof—every scent was richly intoxicating his senses.

An engine screamed as Susan pulled up beside James. She nodded at the moon, which glowed down on them with its silver light, **aloof** to human affairs. It was almost perfectly **effulgent,** and seemed larger than James had ever seen it before. "Full moon tomorrow," Susan shouted over the roar of her engine.

James nodded, unsure how to reply. For some reason, Susan's words had sent a thrill through him.

Susan laughed and sped off, and James found himself laughing

venerate: worship
utilitarian: functional, useful
behemoth: monster or giant
tenuous: feeble or flimsy
subsist: survive
fetid: smelly or rotten
aloof: distant or cold
effulgent: bright or beaming

too, as he followed her. The night was chill, but the breeze still held him like an embrace. He felt like he wasn't even a **terrestrial** being anymore—as if he kept riding long enough, he could soar straight into the sky.

terrestrial: earthly

Chapter Four

Soon there were more buildings and fewer pastures, and soon no pastures at all. The stars seemed to grow dim, and the lights on the horizon grew brighter, and almost immediately after that, James found himself roaring up the highway into the city of London, passing through the **obstreperous** streets of Seven Sisters. It wasn't the kind of neighborhood that James would normally want to visit after dark . . . but with his newfound strength he felt invulnerable. James's life in London had always been so well ordered that it was a **paragon** of British timing and efficiency. He was fascinated to see the other side, the underbelly of the city with its **vibrant** people and their messy, noisy habits. But James had never felt more alive.

Soon they passed the exterior of a club lit with a neon sign that blinked the name Pulse in red letters. James noticed a crowd of good-looking people gathered behind a velvet rope, waiting to get in. Adam motioned for the two vampires to follow him into an alley, where they parked the cycles. Electronica was thumping from behind a brick wall near to them where a large man with a shaved head was standing. This was the rear entrance to the club, and Adam was already striding to the door.

"We're just going to leave the bikes here?" James asked as he pulled off his helmet, fearing that he would have to return to the estate and explain that he had been the victim of **larceny** the first night out with one of Alistair's vehicles. "Shouldn't we park these in a lot somewhere?"

"Don't worry," Adam said smoothly, "Bruce here will keep an eye on things. Won't you, Bruce?" he asked, slapping the guy with the shaved head on the shoulder.

obstreperous: unruly
paragon: ideal or model
vibrant: lively or exciting
larceny: theft

"Right," Bruce said in a South London accent. "And if you have any trouble inside, you can ring me on the dog." Bruce held up a cell phone and flashed James a **canny** smile that wasn't really very reassuring.

"Don't worry," Susan whispered in James's ear as she took him by the arm. "He's much more trustworthy than he looks."

James was relieved by her **candor.** Adam's cocky demeanor was beginning to make James feel like a baby or a dupe who couldn't keep up with a sophisticated **iconoclast** like Adam. "Put on your sunglasses," Susan added as she pulled her dark shades over her eyes. "It's dim inside, but the strobes can bother your **optic** nerve."

James nodded and pulled out his sunglasses—he knew that protecting his vision was **paramount.** A moment later Bruce swung open the door, and James was instantly **pummeled** with the heavy bass of dance music.

Susan laced her fingers through his, leading James through the dark room and onto the dance floor. The room was cavernous, as large as a warehouse, and dark, lit only with flashing strobes and the dim light of glow sticks. The **veracity** of Susan's advice about the sunglasses was proved almost instantly as a flashing light pulsed on and off over James's head. Everywhere beautiful young people moved to the music, writhing **sinuously** on the dance floor as the rhythm carried them away. James felt the music enter his body, and it **inflamed** him.

James began to dance wildly, letting the passion in the music drive him. Susan arched her back, letting her hair spill behind her. James felt the extent of her beauty with an almost physical force. She was the most beautiful woman he had ever seen—she glowed with an **ethereal** beauty that was **unique** . . . yet somehow familiar. In a moment James felt a flash of recognition as he realized that Susan's beauty was like his mother's—cold and almost unreal . . . yet James was sure it was irresistible for most guys.

canny: sly
candor: openness or honesty
iconoclast: someone who disagrees with established beliefs or institutions
optic: relating to sight or the eye
paramount: of greatest importance
pummeled: pounded
veracity: truth
sinuously: in a twisting and turning motion
inflamed: ignited or sparked
ethereal: otherworldly
unique: one of a kind

Already Adam and Susan were attracting attention. Women began to cluster around Adam, their faces transfixed by his magnetic presence. Susan was dancing with a gorgeous dark-skinned man with beautiful, fluid movements.

James turned away from her and found himself dancing with two dark-haired women, both tall and **lithe,** with dancers' bodies. They moved closer to him, dancing **fervently,** and James could feel their hot breath on his skin. Suddenly James's vision began to grow hazy, and his head grew light. The women's faces were near now. One of them had flecks of blue in her hazel eyes, and each fleck appeared to James with the enormity of an entire world, an entire universe. He stumbled away, only to be confronted by another dancing beauty. This one had skin as dark as ebony, and the diamond studs in her earlobes sparkled with the **luminescence** of stars in the night sky. James felt like he was drowning. He had never received so much attention before, and certainly never from such beautiful women. And he felt exhausted by the energy it took to see and feel with his new senses—like he was crushed beneath the heavy **yoke** of their weight. James tried to let his senses go, and the music seemed to come at him from far away. He felt dizzy. He knew that he didn't need air, not anymore, but he still felt oxygen deprived. He wanted to get out. He had to get out. James turned to find the door.

Suddenly, as if appearing from nowhere like a phantom in the night, stood a tall blond woman of striking beauty. Her hair was blond, her eyes bluish green. She looked up at him with a **bashful** glance and began to dance with him. Her movements were slow at first, then began to grow in intensity. James had never felt such a strong attraction to someone before, and the feeling was peculiar and unsettling. He reached out to touch her smooth arm, and his new vampiric senses overwhelmed him. James could smell the warm, coppery scent of her blood. He could almost taste the salt on her skin. But there was more.

lithe: flexible or graceful
fervently: excitedly or passionately
luminescence: light
yoke: burden
bashful: shy

With the touch an image flashed through James's mind. A teakettle, screaming. A gleaming silver toaster. A mug with a chipped rim. A woman. A man. An argument.

James tore his hand away to make the images leave his mind, but it was too late. This girl with the golden blond hair—she had come here tonight to escape an argument. The woman and the man, they were her parents, and this scene was a common one. James also knew what the girl herself knew—that the fight would escalate, that the man would beat the woman until she screamed, begging for him to stop. In an instant James had seen the whole of this golden-haired person's existence—her entire life **recapitulated** in an instant. He saw her family's **impecuniousness,** which kept her mother yoked to a violent, dangerous man. Her mother's **abject** poverty and desperation. Her father's **dominion** over them.

James stared at the girl in shock. *What's happening to me?* he wondered. He blinked once, twice—and the vision evaporated, leaving only the girl bathed in the luminous lights of the club. James didn't know what had happened, but he was certain that what he had seen was real. Could this be another vampire sense? Was he *psychic* now?

James glanced at the girl with all of the **benevolence** he could muster. If all of what he'd seen was true, she was really dealing with a terrible situation.

Just then, she locked his gaze with her own. Her eyes were oceans—their **fecund** depths providing shelter for a million mysteries. She leaned forward and kissed him.

James felt a burst of pleasure as her warm, soft lips met his with a gentle pressure. But this was immediately drowned out by the overwhelming taste of her flesh . . . the smell of her blood filled his nostrils, and the warmth of her body seemed to melt into his. The single taste had awakened a desire in James, and suddenly he was aware of nothing—nothing but his need to feed. It seemed the hun-

recapitulated: summed up
impecuniousness: poverty
abject: miserable
dominion: power or authority
benevolence: kindness or goodwill
fecund: rich or lush

ger would drive everything. It demanded to be **satiated.** James kissed her neck. It took only a moment for him to find the jugular vein.

All around them people continued to dance, oblivious to the crime that was about to take place next to them.

Suddenly the girl looked up at him. He saw her take in the length of his canine teeth. He saw her fear, but she seemed hypnotized. It was at that moment that the **heinousness** of what he was about to do hit James. *No,* he thought, shoving the girl away roughly. ***I ab-jure** this act. I won't do it.*

The girl did not move or cry out as James stumbled away from her, reeling like he was drunk, his head thick and muddled.

James fought his way through the **heterogeneous** throng of beautiful people, all wearing the same blank expression of ecstatic movement, all in fashionable clothing, but ultimately interchange-able. He felt like they could all see what he had almost done—like the mark of his shame was burned **caustically** on his forehead. He was a total **pariah.**

The room seemed to stretch on forever, the throng pulsing to-gether with the beat of the music. Suddenly the relentless music seemed **maudlin,** like a dance of death.

James wandered through the crowd, alone in a sea of people. He wasn't even sure what he was looking for—until he found it.

A series of massive couches hulked in a shadowy corner of the room. The sofas were upholstered with red velvet with luxurious throw pillows and long, low arms. A man and a woman lounged to-gether on one, kissing. The guy pulled back and stared into the woman's eyes. Even from a distance James could see her expres-sion—her eyelids were half closed, almost as though she were hyp-notized as she lay **prostrate** in his arms, obviously overwhelmed by his presence. A few other women lingered nearby, staring at the man with the same hungry expression. They all wanted him. And

satiated: filled or satisfied
heinousness: wickedness or offensiveness
abjure: reject
heterogeneous: mixed or assorted
caustically: sharply
pariah: outsider or reject
maudlin: weepy or overemotional
prostrate: horizontal

when he touched the woman's throat, tracing a finger across her white neck, the other women sighed, and their lids dropped slightly as they imagined themselves in her place.

James stood there, transfixed by the scene. The guy on the couch was Adam.

Adam ran his hand across the woman's shoulders, lightly moving his fingers across the strap of the silver halter she wore over a hip-slung mini, which **accentuated** her flat belly. Her eyes fluttered. Adam grinned as she arched her back and pulled Adam toward her for a kiss. He finally **acquiesced,** in an **elaborate parody** of passion. James winced. This was disgusting—Adam's touch only **defiled** her. He gazed up and down her body in an appraising, almost **officious** way. But his gaze stopped at her neck. It was as though James could see the places where Adam had touched her arms in streaks that **defaced** her beauty. James found the whole scene **odious,** but just like the other night with Francis, somehow he couldn't do anything to stop it or even turn away. It was as though Adam had **fettered** him, just as he had fettered the woman on the couch.

Adam touched her neck and her body responded with an involuntary shudder. She couldn't resist Adam. And James knew that she wouldn't escape him.

Almost as though he could feel the **wrath** that rolled off James in waves, Adam looked up. His eyes held James's for a moment, and he gave an **imperious** grin. He held James's gaze as he brushed the black hair away from her white neck. It only took a moment for him to sink his teeth into the woman's flesh.

She still had no idea of the **egregious** mistake she had made. She was letting him feed on her, and she had no clue that she was dying. James was amazed at how **efficacious** physical attraction could be in overpowering the normal human senses. It **obscured** all reason and rendered a normally **acute** person **obtuse.**

Adam stood up, letting the woman slump against the low arm of

accentuated: drew attention
acquiesced: gave in
elaborate: complex or drawn out
parody: imitation or mockery
defiled: ruined or dirtied
officious: impertinent
defaced: spoiled
odious: horrible
fettered: chained
wrath: anger
imperious: arrogant or domineering
egregious: glaring or obvious
efficacious: effective
obscured: hid
acute: sharp or perceptive
obtuse: stupid or simpleminded

the couch. Her eyes were closed and she was smiling. It looked as though she were passed out, as though she had just been left by a **fickle** boyfriend to peacefully sleep off the **bliss** they had shared. But James knew the truth.

In an instant James was released from whatever spell had held him as the hideous scene flooded over him. "No!" he shouted, but his voice was lost in the beat of the music.

Adam looked over at him again and smiled his **scurrilous** smile.

James looked around frantically, unsure what to do. *Find Susan,* his mind whispered. *Find Susan.* Yes, yes. Susan. James lurched away through the crowd, silently **berating** himself for not having stopped Adam. *You **abetted** his crime,* he told himself harshly. *In doing nothing, you're just as guilty as he is!*

He **canvassed** the rear of the club but couldn't find Susan anywhere. The warehouse was **capacious**—it was going to be nearly impossible to find her, James realized with dismay. Instead he settled on a new plan. The exit was only **accessible** down a long hallway at the far end of the space. He stumbled toward it.

James pulled out of the crowd and took a **circuitous** path around the edge of the room to arrive at the hallway. Just before he reached it, he caught sight of Susan's auburn hair. For a moment James was **elated.** But his joy quickly dissipated when he realized that she was kissing the dark-skinned man James had seen her with earlier. No—he realized with growing horror—she wasn't kissing him. . . .

Susan turned and looked at James. A small bead of blood trickled from the corner of her mouth. The man's eyes closed, and he slumped in the corner.

James's body was flooded with **distaste.** He ran toward the exit. He felt faint; he had to get out of there.

James burst through the exit doors and staggered into the alley.

"You okay, mate?" Bruce asked as James lurched away.

"No," James croaked. He didn't care if he was guilty of some kind

fickle: unpredictable or unreliable
bliss: pleasure or delight
scurrilous: vulgar or offensive
berating: criticizing
abetted: assisted or supported
canvassed: patrolled
capacious: large
accessible: reachable
circuitous: winding or indirect
elated: excited or overjoyed
distaste: disgust

of effrontery. He just wanted to be left alone. He had no desire to stand there and chat with a **gregarious** bouncer—he was feeling sick, like he had been poisoned. It was all he could do to haul himself into a corner, where he tried to vomit. But nothing would come up. He had to lean against the brick wall to hold himself up.

Music blared and receded as the door flew open, then swung shut again.

"I think your mate is sick," Bruce said.

"We know," Susan's voice replied.

James heard two sets of footsteps come up behind him.

"What the hell is your problem?" Adam demanded. His voice was harsh, like sandpaper, and it grated on James's nerves.

Suddenly all of the **latent** anger that had been simmering in James began to boil over. "You want to know what my problem is?" James demanded, turning to face Adam. His voice wasn't loud, but it was hard as steel. "You killed them," he whispered. His glance drifted from Adam to Susan, who looked away, then back again. "You killed them," he said again, slightly louder this time.

Adam's hand shot out and he pinned James against the wall. "Watch the **defamatory** remarks," he growled through gritted teeth. He turned to Bruce and said, "Could we have a little privacy, mate?"

"Sure, sure," Bruce muttered, and disappeared inside the rear door.

Adam turned back to James. "Pull yourself together," he commanded. "Do you want to ruin everything?" His gray eyes flashed cold, like steel.

James saw Adam's lips moving, but he wasn't comprehending his words. *I can't do it,* he thought. *I can't kill people.* "I'm not like you," he whispered.

"I'm not like you," Adam repeated, mocking him **impudently.** He narrowed his eyes, obviously disgusted by James's **mawkish** concern for human beings. "Of course you're not!" He gave James a fi-

gregarious: social or talkative
latent: hidden or buried
defamatory: insulting or slanderous
impudently: insolently
mawkish: overemotional

nal shove, then turned and stalked to his motorcycle. The engine screamed as he roared off into the streets of London.

James's head swam; he couldn't think. Images were coming to him slowly and indistinctly. He slid down the wall until he was sitting on the ground in the alley.

"Are you all right?" Susan asked gently. She crouched to put a hand on his arm.

Even this **nominal** kindness nearly undid James. He looked up at Susan, wishing that her eyes weren't hidden behind dark sunglasses. "Why?" he choked out.

"'Death, as the Psalmist saith, is certain to all; all shall die,'" Susan said.

"That's a **maxim** I've never heard," James said bitterly.

"It's from Shakespeare," Susan replied. "The **immortal bard** himself."

"I've always believed in just living and letting people live," James told her.

"Look, you can't feel guilty about killing a human being," Susan explained. She picked up James's hand and laced her fingers through his. James marveled at how she could make something so horrible sound like an **innocuous** statement. But she went on, "You shouldn't feel any more guilty for feeding on a human than a human would feel for eating bacon or chicken. Humans are food, and we're as far removed from them on the food chain as they are from . . . well . . . **escargot.**" She smiled a little at her joke and went on. "We're immortal, James," she whispered. "And that makes us special."

James shook his head. "I'm sorry," he said, "I just don't see it that way."

"Neither did I," Susan told him. "I felt exactly the same way you do—in the beginning. Then Adam and Alistair showed me the truth. You'll see it, too, one day."

nominal: small or insignificant
maxim: saying
immortal: undying
bard: poet
innocuous: harmless
escargot: snails

James didn't bother to reply. He knew Susan would never understand how he thought, just like he couldn't begin to understand what she was saying.

Susan glanced at her watch. "It's almost four," she said. "We don't want to be caught on the cycles at sunrise. We'd go blind even with the helmet visors."

James nodded, thinking about the nasty burn he knew he could get from the sun. He struggled to haul himself to his feet. But when he finally stood, he could hardly move. He tried to take a step and stumbled. Susan caught him before he fell.

"You have to feed," Susan said, looking at him closely. "Tomorrow's the full moon—it's the last day of the cycle."

"But I fed—" James protested.

"When?"

James shook his head, trying to think. "When I became a vampire . . ."

"First Feed isn't nourishing," Susan insisted. "The feed when you become a vampire—when they take your blood and you take theirs—only replaces what's been lost. You have to feed soon after that."

"What are you saying?" James's eyes were wide.

Susan's glance flickered to the rear door of the club.

"No." James's voice was firm.

"If you don't feed, you'll die."

Then let me die. How could he not die, if existing meant preying on other people? It went against everything in his nature. He couldn't do it. He wouldn't. . . .

Just then a trim woman in her mid-thirties walked by the alley. She peered inside, and for a moment her eyes locked with James's. James took in everything about her in a single glance—the yoga pants, the terry jacket, the sneakers. She looked like a Chelsea professional who had wandered far past her territory. James wondered what she was doing in Seven Sisters but guessed she must live in the neighborhood. She was clearly out for her morning exercise, walking her German shepherd. And she was pulsing with life. James's vampiric vision was filled with her energy, the beating of her blood.

In that instant he could smell the warm scent of her flesh, smell the blood that filled her veins. All thoughts of his own death fled his mind as he focused on her life. Dimly his reluctance to kill throbbed in his mind, but James had already taken a step toward her. *This is wrong*, he thought. But the hunger . . . it was making him desperate. He took another tentative step.

"Do it," Susan whispered.

In one fluid motion James descended.

The woman screamed as James sank his teeth into the neck of the German shepherd. She kept screaming as James drained the dog's blood. The dog fell to the ground, and James took one quick glance at the woman's distraught face and hurried away.

Susan was already astride her bike. James ran to his motorcycle and revved the engine, and a moment later he was roaring after Susan, tearing down the deserted city streets.

James realized with a sudden flash of insight that his head was finally clear. The blood had helped him—although it had not wholly satiated him.

Buildings whipped past until finally he and Susan hit the suburbs and then the open road. The sky was beginning to lighten to gray and would soon be pink with the warmish predawn glow. James and Susan poured on the speed. He was pretty sure that they'd make it to the manor in time, but was that even something to be grateful for?

When his own mother turned him into this . . . this *thing*, he'd been given a life sentence. A life sentence and a death sentence, all in one.

Chapter Five

James woke up to a dark room. Not a ray of light shone from the cracks at the corners of the velvet blackout curtains that covered the leaded glass windows. James sat up, feeling better than he had in days. He gave an involuntary shudder when he realized that this was probably because of the blood he drank the night before.

James crossed to the window and flung the curtains wide. He peered out into the dark night in a **vain** effort to **abort** the memories from the night before that were already **deluging** him. He wondered how Susan and Adam could be so **impervious** to the knowledge that their lives depended on others' deaths. What sort of tricks did they have to play on their minds, what sort of **legerdemain** of reason did they have to practice in order to keep up the farce that this was their right, as supernatural beings?

James took one last look out the window. Almost overnight the air had turned from chill to frosty, and the leaves had begun to change color. James could detect minute changes in the life light of the leaves. **Ominous** clouds darkened half the sky, **obliterating** the stars behind. The last **vestiges** of the **verdant** summer were disappearing, making way for the more **parsimonious**, **austere** beauty of winter.

James walked down the stairs, but he didn't find Susan in the kitchen. She wasn't in the study, either. *She must be out, **cavorting** with Adam,* James thought bitterly. He couldn't explain his **bias** against Adam, but he couldn't deny it, either. It was just that James had the sense that Adam was completely alien—a being **bereft** of human feelings. And that made him very, very dangerous.

As he strode past Alistair's study, James heard a soft, **melodious**

vain: useless
abort: stop or terminate
deluging: overwhelming, swamping
impervious: resistant
legerdemain: trick or sleight of hand
ominous: threatening
obliterating: covering or causing to disappear
vestiges: traces or remnants
verdant: green
parsimonious: stingy or miserly
austere: somber or stark
cavorting: horsing around
bias: prejudice or favoritism
bereft: lacking or without
melodious: beautiful or harmonious

voice from behind the closed door. Then another, lower voice followed—a **medley** of sound. The voices were whispered but intense. The words were **indistinct,** so James leaned closer. He couldn't be sure, but he thought he heard his name. **Impulsively** James turned the handle and swung open the door.

Alistair and Adam looked up, and Adam's mouth closed like a trap.

"Speak of the devil," Alistair said smoothly.

James hesitated in the doorway. "Were you talking about me?"

"Adam was just telling me about your trip into the city," Alistair said. "Thank you, Adam. You may go."

Conscious of his place in the **hierarchy,** and perhaps of his dependence on his **benefactor**'s **largesse,** Adam rose and gave Alistair a **deferential** nod before stalking to the door. Although he didn't even glance at James on his way out, James could feel the searing heat of Adam's hostility from across the room.

"Sit down," Alistair commanded.

In a desire to be **accommodating,** James **complied.** He somehow didn't want to offend the elegant older vampire, as ludicrous as that was considering who—or what—Alistair was. Besides, he was probably in for a lecture **imputing** him for his irresponsible, cowardly actions the night before.

Alistair leaned back comfortably in his overstuffed wingback chair. **Medieval** weapons gleamed on the wall behind him as he said, "The existence of a vampire is an **onerous** one, wouldn't you say, James?"

"Sir?" James asked. He didn't want to be **impertinent,** but he wasn't really following Alistair. The last thing he'd expected was for him to be **lenient**, after all the big talk about vampire power.

"It seems, James, that I owe you an apology." Alistair's teeth gleamed in the low light cast from the fireplace as he smiled softly. James's eyes wandered across the spines of **tome** after tome that

medley: jumble or mix
indistinct: vague or muffled
impulsively: hastily or without thought
hierarchy: ranking chain of command
benefactor: sponsor
largesse: generosity or aid
deferential: respectful
accommodating: cooperative or helpful
complied: obeyed
imputing: accusing or blaming
medieval: from the middle ages (500–1500 A.D.)
onerous: difficult
impertinent: impolite or disrespectful
lenient: merciful
tome: book

lined Alistair's shelves, and he wondered whether the old vampire had read all of these books. In a life span of more than three hundred fifty years, he might have. "In making my decision to allow Adam to be your escort on your first slay, I'm afraid I acted **capriciously.** The idea of feeding on humans can **elicit** a strong response in a new vampire; I should have remembered that. I don't know why I expected you to take to the hunt immediately when in fact most vampires don't. Many try to maintain their **fidelity** to human values for a long time after the Change. Someone who is used to a certain **rectitude** can't **reconcile** his new existence with his old one overnight."

James leaned forward on the couch, trying to follow what Alistair was saying. There was something about the lilt of Alistair's voice, especially combined with the low, flickering light in the room and the sweet smell that emanated from the fireplace, that was having a **soporific** effect on James. It was practically **lulling** him to sleep.

"But it is important for vampires to get over their misplaced feelings of pity," Alistair went on. "For example, what would have happened, James, if you had stopped Adam from feeding the night before? Last night was Final Phase—the moon has passed into full. If Adam had not fed, he would be dead now. Or even worse, what if you had called for help? If the police had arrived and tried to arrest Adam, let me assure you, there would be a number of dead policemen to account for. Human strength is incredibly **meager** compared to that of a vampire. They would not have stood a chance. And—finally—what if you had interrupted Adam in his feed? What if the girl had lived and had gone on to become a vampire? What kind of existence would you have **bequeathed** her? And how many other human deaths would have resulted from your actions?" Alistair leaned forward and fixed James with an intense gaze. "New vampires are **notorious** for their good intentions," he said. "I admire your principles, James, but I **beseech** you to think about what

capriciously: impulsively or without thought
elicit: bring out
fidelity: loyalty or devotion
rectitude: goodness or morality
reconcile: resolve or fit
soporific: sleep inducing
lulling: calming or quieting
meager: small or insufficient
bequeathed: given
notorious: infamous
beseech: beg or plead

you might have done. This is nothing more than sentimentality. We aren't like them," he whispered. "We don't live by their ethics. A vampire must be what it is. It cannot be anything else."

James stared into the black **void** of Alistair's eyes, feeling lost in their depth. Part of his mind whispered that there was something **depraved** in this speech, but the crazy thing was, it actually made sense. What had seemed right the night before seemed all twisted around now. Of course, a vampire must be what it was. How could it be otherwise?

In a flash James remembered Francis. The cruel lines of his face, the harsh edge of his arguments. Maybe the world was better off without Francis. Maybe that was why Alistair had chosen him as a victim. . . .

"You don't seem like someone who believes in **abnegation**," Alistair said in his cool voice.

"No," James agreed. His tongue felt thick, like he'd been drugged. He struggled to form the words. "No, of course not."

"You can't feed on lower life-forms forever, James. A vampire needs human blood. But you don't have to feed on the young and beautiful—you don't even have to feed on the good. Think about that, James. We have the power—no, the responsibility—to choose who lives and who dies. That is a power that can be used wisely or foolishly. I'll take you on the next slay personally. And I promise that you'll find it a great deal more appealing than Adam's butchery." Alistair tapped his long, tapered fingers against the rich brown leather of the chair's arm. "I never should have trusted Adam with a charge like this."

James nodded, his body flooding with relief. Somehow he believed Alistair. With him "the slay" would be done right. Not such a **cynical**, mocking act. **Reflexively** James drew his hand across his forehead.

"Everything all right?" Alistair asked.

void: emptiness
depraved: evil or corrupt
abnegation: self-denial
cynical: sneering or mocking
reflexively: without thinking

James shook his head. "It's just—I had these dreams. And last night I touched a woman . . . and it was almost like I was inside her mind. . . ." He looked at Alistair closely to see if the older vampire understood what he was trying to say, but Alistair's expression was **inscrutable.** "I saw things, and I was sure that I was seeing what she had seen. . . ."

Alistair's eyebrows lifted **minutely.** "And the dream?"

James shook his head. "Pain. A white room. A strange light . . ." He bit his lip, concentrating, but he couldn't recall more. "Mostly what I remember is the pain. Inhuman pain."

"I see." Alistair pressed his fingertips together, forming a steeple. "Very interesting . . ." He stood up. "I think, perhaps, that we should go on our hunt soon. Possibly even before the next Final Phase. I'll make the arrangements." He nodded at James, who understood that he was being dismissed.

"Thank you, Alistair."

Alistair waved his hand. "This is what I'm here for."

James retreated from the study, back up to his room. He needed to think about what Alistair had said. But it made sense to **defer** to the older vampire's wisdom, didn't it?

When James pushed open the door to his room, he was surprised to see Susan standing by the window, gazing through the rippled glass at the nocturnal scene below.

Susan looked up as James walked in. She held something white in her hand.

"I have a letter for you," Susan said, holding out the envelope.

"A letter?" James frowned as he took it from her. He hadn't received a real piece of written **correspondence** in years. It felt solid and comforting in his fingers. He flipped it over. At the upper-right corner was the familiar image of the queen. And below, at the center of the page, was Alistair's address. James felt a lump form in his throat at the sight of the handwriting. It was from his mother. He

inscrutable: hard to read or interpret
minutely: slightly
defer: submit or give in
correspondence: mail or communication

folded the letter and stuffed it into a pocket. He didn't know if he could handle reading what she had to say to him, but he definitely couldn't read it with Susan there.

"Vampires never use e-mail for anything important," Susan explained. "It's too easy for someone sniffing the Web to get information. Besides, the screens—"

"Bother our eyes." James nodded. Of course. And private mail was protected by law. Strangely, it was more private than anything high-tech. "Susan—" James began, but she held up her hand.

"Don't," she said. "I want you to know that I think what you did is completely honorable."

James lifted his eyebrows in surprise. He hadn't expected anything like that from her. "No," James said quietly, thinking of his conversation with Alistair. "What I did was cowardly. I **endangered** us all."

"Maybe," Susan admitted. "But it's been a long time since I've seen a vampire try to be merciful," she went on, staring at the floor. "I'd forgotten that it was possible." She turned and stepped through the door. Her footsteps made no noise as she hurried down the hall.

James stared after her for a moment, then pulled out his mother's letter. He sat down on the bed and opened the envelope carefully, his whole body tight with tension. He'd always had mixed feelings about his mother—wishing she could be normal, like his friends' mums, but loving her all the same. Now he didn't know what to feel. Part of him wanted to rip up the letter and toss it right in the trash. But he knew he couldn't. He had to know what had made her do this to him.

Darling James, he read.

I don't know whether you can ever forgive me, but I hope that you understand why I did what I did. By now you will know the truth about me and the truth about yourself, and it is my

endangered: put at risk

greatest wish that you can put yourself in my shoes and think about why I had to do it. You aren't a mother, so you can't possibly understand what it's like to want the best for your son. But I swear, I know what is best, and this is best. I admit that I was partially motivated by my own selfish reasons, reasons that deserve no ***accolades****, but I could not imagine an immortal existence in which I lived to watch my own son grow old and die before me while I enjoyed* ***eternal*** *youth. Not while it was in my power to change that.*

Please, listen to Alistair. He is very wise and very powerful, and he can help you. But please, please, be careful.

All my love,
Angelica

She had enclosed a photo. James looked at it, remembering the day it was taken. They had spent the afternoon at the zoo. His mother had bought him a balloon, but James hadn't held it carefully, and it sailed up into the sky. He had cried until she bought him another one. And there it was in the photo, attached to his arm in a slipknot, as he and his mother grinned and squinted into the camera.

James stared at the photo for a moment, wondering why she had chosen to send this one. There were definitely better images of both of them in the house. There was something strange about this photo. . . . It took James a full minute to realize what it was. They were standing in the broad daylight. The sun was so bright, in fact, that they had to squint, but his mother wasn't wearing sunglasses.

She wasn't a vampire then, James realized suddenly.

But what did it mean? James was almost positive that his mother was trying to send him a message . . . something beyond what she'd said in her letter.

But what on earth could it possibly be?

accolades: praise or compliments

eternal: endless

* * * * *

When James woke up, he was in a white room. But there was something wrong with his vision. Images seemed **distorted** and strange, twisted almost beyond recognition. James wondered whether the problem was with his sight or with his mind. He tried to move his body so that he could see better, but he was **immobile,** held down by something. His heart gave an involuntary flutter, more like a shudder, as it thudded hard against his rib cage, sending him into a **vortex** of unreasonable fear. James couldn't say why he was afraid, but the fear captured him and **captivated** him. James just wished that he could understand the fear, because he knew that an unnamed anxiety could be the most **deleterious.**

Slowly and **deliberately,** James looked around. He forced himself to take in details, even though his vision was weak, like a **flaccid** muscle that hadn't been used for weeks. His heart still thudding in his ears, he saw the smooth lines of a white flower from his **peripheral** vision. Then a strange glow, as though from light **refracted** through water. James thought of tranquil seas, diving underwater and being surrounded by a flashing cloud of silversides. . . .

"No, please, no more. . . ."

The voice was a quiet murmur, but James felt his own lips moving. The words were his, but what did they mean? For a moment nothing **elucidated** them.

Then came the pain.

James writhed in **anguish** as blinding pain tore through his body. The quiet voice again used James's lips to beg for mercy, but there was no reply. James was confused by the **vicarious** experience, momentarily unable to distinguish where his pain began and the pain of the other—James was sure now that there was someone else, that this wasn't actually happening to him at all—ended.

The pain stopped, and James caught his breath, then it **accosted**

distorted: twisted or deformed
immobile: fixed or motionless
vortex: whirlpool
captivated: fascinated
deleterious: harmful
deliberately: carefully or slowly
flaccid: limp or flabby
peripheral: on the side
refracted: bent rays of light
elucidated: explained or made clear
anguish: pain or agony
vicarious: lived or experienced through another person
accosted: confronted or attacked

him again. But what was causing it? James couldn't see his attacker. Now and then he thought he caught sight of something—a **scintillating** dark eye?—only to have the vision disappear before he could be sure.

The agony went on and on, its **accretion** reaching **unfathomable** levels. James had only felt pain this intense once before, on the night he became a vampire. But this was worse. He felt like he was journeying to the edge of death itself. . . .

Suddenly the pain stopped. James opened his eyes and sat up. The mysterious **pathology** that had clouded his vision had gone away entirely, and he could see perfectly. But he was no longer in the white room. He was in his room, surrounded by the same **opulent** antique furniture that he had been that morning when he went to bed. *It was just a dream,* James told himself.

He shivered, then noticed the thin sliver of light that was creeping in at the corner of the heavy blackout curtains that lined his windows. It was the middle of the day—he still had hours to sleep. James cringed and got up to arrange the curtain, wondering about his nightmare. Even though part of him wanted to believe that dreams were nothing but fascinating nonsense, he couldn't help believing that this dream was more—that the mixture of symbols and emotions had meaning and that it was James's duty to decode them. He wasn't sure whether this dream had anything to do with being a vampire. But his gut told him it did. *I'll have to ask Alistair,* James thought, wishing he wasn't such an ignorant **novice** about all of this.

James's hand shook as he drew the curtain across the light, then returned to his bed. He felt exhausted, his mind **torpid.** He couldn't translate his fevered dream. Not tonight, anyway.

As James crawled beneath the thick down of the duvet, his eye fell on the bedside table, landing on the photograph his mother had sent. James picked it up, thinking about what his mother had writ-

scintillating: brilliant or dazzling
accretion: buildup
unfathomable: unknowable or unbelievable
pathology: irregularity or abnormality
opulent: fancy or lavish
novice: beginner
torpid: lazy

ten. Her letter had a strangely **abridged** quality, as though she had written it in a hurry . . . or perhaps as though she wanted to say more than she could. *Or,* James thought bitterly, *maybe because she was being* **mendacious***. She didn't want what was best for me. She wanted what was best for herself.* Angelica didn't want anything to **impinge** on her perfect life. She sure didn't want her son to have the normal human life that she had given up. And so she had **abrogated** that life and given him a new one. The same one she had chosen for herself.

James shoved the photo into a drawer. He couldn't look at it anymore. He was tired. Just so tired.

James lay back and tried to sleep. He had to get his rest . . . it would be sundown soon.

abridged: shortened
mendacious: false or misleading

impinge: intrude

abrogated: undone or canceled

Chapter Six

"Researching your memoirs?" James joked as he walked into the library, where Susan sat reading a book on the history of vampires.

Susan didn't laugh. She looked up at him with strangely vacant eyes, then looked down at her book again. James noticed that her fine bone-white skin was lined and creased at the corners of her mouth.

James could tell that she wanted to be alone, but he didn't want to leave. He had barely seen Susan at all in the past few days, and he was worried that she'd been avoiding him. And he didn't want her to avoid him. Adam was so **mercurial,** and Alistair so unapproachable, that James felt Susan was his only shot at a real friend. He took a single, **timorous** step toward her, then gained courage and sat down beside her on the sofa.

"Alistair is taking me on a slay tonight," James said slowly. His voice sounded **inane** to his own ears, so he wasn't surprised when Susan looked at him sharply.

"What?" she whispered.

"On a slay," James repeated.

Susan frowned. "But you think it's wrong."

For a moment James was flabbergasted. He had expected Susan to be proud that James had finally come to his senses. Part of him was angry at Susan's response to this **seminal** event. It would be the night that James would be **indoctrinated** as a vampire. He would taste real human blood for the first time. First Feed didn't count—that was only his own blood returning to his body. This slay would be real. Alistair had convinced him that it was possible to kill mercifully, and James was eager to see how it was done.

mercurial: inconstant, changeable
timorous: nervous or shy
inane: silly or stupid
seminal: formative or decisive
indoctrinated: taught the fundamentals

Susan's eyes clouded over as she whispered, "Don't go."

"What?"

"Don't go." Susan's forehead was etched with concern. "You don't have to. You can take another animal—"

"Alistair says that the reason I've been so lethargic lately is because I need human blood," James replied. But this was only half of the truth. Alistair had also told James that he couldn't master his vampire abilities until he had tasted human blood. James had been unable to get the strange dream he'd had several days before out of his mind. He wanted to be able to translate its **figurative** system of symbols into **rational** thoughts, and he was sure if he could control his vampire senses, he could decode the dream.

"James, I don't think you understand." Susan's face paled as she spoke. "I used to think like you. Until that night—the night that you chose not to kill a human. I had never thought of it as murder before, but now . . ." She looked around and then leaned toward James closely, her voice dropping to a whisper. "Look, there are things you don't know about Alistair—"

"Well, I see that we're getting very cozy," Adam said in his deep, masculine voice as he swaggered into the library. He didn't even glance in James's direction as he draped himself across the arm of the couch. He picked up a lock of Susan's hair and toyed with it absently. Susan swatted his hand away. Adam **feigned** hurt. "In a foul temper, are we?" he murmured soothingly. "Perhaps I have something that can cheer you up." He leaned toward Susan and whispered something in her ear.

James strained to hear the words but caught nothing.

Susan's eyelids dropped half closed. James wondered what Adam was saying. Whatever it was, his **oration** was having an intense effect on Susan.

After a moment she looked up at Adam. The expression on her face had changed completely, the mistrust and concern replaced by

figurative: symbolic

rational: based on reason or logic

feigned: faked or simulated

oration: speech

excitement and, perhaps, James thought, dread. "Where?" Susan's voice was a hoarse whisper.

"In the study," Adam replied. And then he took her hand.

James hovered behind as Adam led Susan across the hall to Alistair's study, where two young olive-skinned women were seated on the couch. They were twins, and both had long, lush black hair that fell to their waists and full, **sensuous** lips. Their large, dark eyes gave them an air of **pathos** as they looked up at Adam, and James instantly felt sorry for them. It was clear as they cast adoring glances at Adam, as their lips parted in desire for him, that they would be completely **tractable.** They were hypnotized by his presence . . . and they had no idea what he was.

Adam sat down between the women. He turned to one and stroked her shoulder, and she let out a sigh. Then he leaned over and whispered **blandishments** in her ear. James couldn't hear the words, but he could imagine them. He wondered vaguely what **vicissitudes** had brought them here. How had these girls met Adam? How had they stumbled across the man who would cause their death?

Adam looked up and smiled at Susan.

But Susan hung back, merely watching as Adam traced a **tortuous** route along the neck of the other twin with his fingertip. James wondered why Susan didn't join Adam. Only a few weeks ago she had been his partner in exactly this sort of **licentious** scene—why did she resist it now? James wasn't sure how to feel. He knew that he should feel glad that Susan was **abstaining** from slaying one of the twins. But another part of him felt the hunger . . . felt the excitement of holding another person's life in his hands. Susan's own words—that vampires were **immortal** and thus special—rang in his ears. He thought about the eagerness with which he had looked forward to tonight's slay with Alistair and wondered why he had ever been so eager to be merciful. Suddenly James wondered what line

sensuous: luscious or fleshy
pathos: sadness
tractable: obedient
blandishments: flattering words
vicissitudes: events or circumstances
tortuous: winding
licentious: immoral
abstaining: refraining or avoiding
immortal: undying

delineated mercy from right—he could no longer **catalog** his reasons for not wanting to kill; every single argument eluded him. He wanted one of these girls. And none of his **cerebral** arguments for morality seemed to matter anymore in the face of the two **sensual** creatures that were seated on the couch before him. . . .

James looked at Susan and knew that she was struggling with the same hunger he was. She took a step forward. Adam leered at her wolfishly, and she froze. In an instant her face turned pale, and she rushed out of the room.

James watched her go, feeling like he was waking from a vivid dream. He turned back to where Adam sat on the couch. His smile faltered as Susan's footsteps retreated down the hallway. But a moment later one of the twins reached for him, and he was instantly absorbed in lavishing attention on them once again.

In a flash James felt white-hot fury coursing through his veins as he realized that all of the arguments that Alistair had given him in favor of killing were actually a form of **demagoguery.** Alistair was **biased** against humans—he saw himself as better than they were, so he felt justified in killing them. But a person wasn't the same thing as an animal raised for slaughter. These young girls on the couch had their whole lives ahead of them. They were **sentient** and self-aware. They knew fear . . . and they knew hope. Killing them was **flagrantly** wrong. Susan was obviously coming to terms with this idea—that was what she had been trying to tell him earlier in the library, James was sure of it. And James knew that she was right. Adam was going to kill these girls. And James couldn't let Adam do it.

"Stop it," James hissed. "Stop it!" He stepped over to the couch and tore one of the girls away from Adam, who looked up at James and snarled. The girl reached for Adam again, and James shoved her away. Adam stared at him, his expression full of rage. "Why do you have to feed on them?" James demanded, looking down at the

delineated: defined or separated
catalog: list
cerebral: logical or intellectual
sensual: animal or carnal
demagoguery: leadership by false promises
biased: unfair or prejudiced
sentient: conscious, aware
flagrantly: obviously or glaringly

young, **unblemished** girls before him. One of them traced her finger along James's knee, but he batted her hand away, **incensed** by her gesture. "Why don't you feed on someone old or sick? Someone who would die, anyway?"

But Adam didn't flinch beneath James's **tirade.** "Mind your own business, Weston," he said, and then turned back to the girls.

"Stop it!" James shouted again. The scene before him was **noxious**; it actually turned his stomach.

With one **deft** movement Adam stood up and slapped James across the face, sending him reeling backward. "You think you're so merciful," Adam spat. "You and Alistair—you're so **scrupulous**, aren't you? Feed on the sick and the old—what a solution! You're ready to **vilify** me when you don't even know what you're talking about!"

James held his stinging cheek as he stared up at Adam, who had gone through a complete **metamorphosis.** A moment ago he had been all sensuality. But now he was a creature driven by rage.

Adam shook his head, disgust stamped across his face. "When are you going to learn that there's no such thing as a merciful vampire?" He crossed to the door at the rear of the study so quickly that James didn't see the movement. But in a flash the door was open. "Look at this! This is what a real vampire does, Weston!"

A woman lay across a bed, seemingly asleep. Her skin was pale and made even paler by the white sheets and walls that surrounded her. She was so thin that she appeared **emaciated.** Her breathing was shallow. Still, there was no obvious evidence that she had been mistreated. Next to the bed was a table, on which lay a tray of food, a glass of water, a lamp, and a vase of white flowers. But James saw the thin gold chain that ran from her ankle and ended at the bedpost, where it was bolted securely, and he understood its **implications** immediately. The girl was food. Vampire food.

"Believe me," Adam said as he looked at the girl, "the girls on the

unblemished: perfect or pure
incensed: angered
tirade: outburst
noxious: disgusting or offensive
deft: nimble or quick
scrupulous: moral or proper
vilify: speak poorly of
metamorphosis: transformation or change
emaciated: thin or shrunken
implications: meanings or consequences

couch are lucky."

Inarticulate rage coursed through James's body. His eyes switched to the bedside, where the glass of water glowed strangely beside the lamp. The white flowers . . . tulips . . . he recognized them. He recognized this pristine white room. This was the girl in his nightmares—the one who begged for mercy with James's lips. *Adam has been draining her slowly,* James realized. *She's chained to the bed so that she can't escape and become a vampire herself.*

Without thinking, James lunged forward to try to rip the chain from the bed.

"What the hell do you think you're doing?" Adam shouted. He grabbed James's collar, but James elbowed him in the **sternum,** then landed a hard blow against Adam's cheekbone. Adam stumbled backward, overturning the table. The lamp landed on the floor with a crash, and the girl's eyes fluttered open. James knelt beside the bed.

"Do I know you?" she asked weakly.

"No," James said quietly. "But I know you."

The girl didn't seem confused by this statement; she just nodded and held James's gaze. "Your eyes are kind," she murmured. Her eyelids dropped closed, and for a moment James thought she might have fallen asleep again. But then she whispered, "End it."

James felt cold at the request. End it . . . She wanted to die. Still, James hesitated. *What did I expect?* he **berated** himself. *That I would* ***abscond*** *with this girl and take her—where? Her only choice is to die or become a vampire.* Besides, James had to think about all of the other humans who would then die at this girl's hands. He couldn't do it. *End it* . . . The words echoed in his mind, and James knew that he would have to acquiesce.

Slowly James bent over the girl. His lips brushed her neck for a split second before he sank his teeth into her tender flesh. Warm blood coursed into his mouth, and the moment the thick, salty liq-

inarticulate: speechless or incoherent

sternum: breastbone

berated: criticized

abscond: run away

uid landed on his tongue, James felt stronger. It didn't take long to drain her. He drank until the girl sank back against the pillows. When he drew away, he knew that she was dead.

James sank to his haunches and skittered backward, away from the dead girl. *I killed her,* he thought, *I killed her!* He had tasted her blood, and he had become a murderer. But the worst part was, he had liked it. No, more than that, he had needed it. Now that he had tasted human blood, he felt the weakness of the animal blood he'd fed on before. And he felt its **paucity.** A dog was small compared to a human, and human blood was so much richer. . . .

Behind him, Adam was struggling to his feet. He stared at James, then gaped at the girl on the bed. In a moment his face flushed **florid.** "What did you do?" he screamed, rushing at James. "You're dead!"

James met the attack head-on, and the two vampires collided with the violence of an explosive locomotive crash. They stumbled out of the white room and back into the study, where Adam's foot caught the **ornately** carved leg of the sofa and sent him sprawling. James leapt at him, blinded by rage. He had just tasted fresh blood, and his senses were overwhelmed with it. He couldn't think of anything else except for how much he **despised** Adam and how badly he wanted to hurt him.

But Adam was a **redoubtable** opponent. He deflected James's blow and leapt to his feet. With speed even faster than James's vampire sight could follow, Adam flew to the wall that held Alistair's weapons and grabbed a dangerous-looking **implement.** Then, throwing all the power of his **brawn** behind the movement, he charged at James.

James turned so that the full weight of the blow caught only the side of his shoulder. But pain ripped across his flesh as he felt the dagger tear at his bicep. He lashed out as quickly as he could and managed to send the dagger flying out of Adam's hand. It skittered

paucity: lack or small amount of
florid: red or ruddy
ornately: richly or elaborately
despised: hated
redoubtable: fearsome or mighty
implement: tool or instrument
brawn: strength or brute force

across the floor. Reflexively James lifted his hand to the wound to stop the bleeding, but when he pulled his hand away, he saw that the bleeding had stopped, and the wound was already healing.

But James should have been watching Adam more **vigilantly.** During the brief moment in which James was distracted by his wound, Adam attacked and sent James crashing against the wall of weapons. The ancient knives and axes fell down around him like iron rain. Adam wrapped his hands around James's throat and began to twist.

His right hand flailing, James reached out toward the wall behind him. Pain raked across his fingers, and he knew he had something. A long, thin-bladed knife. Awkwardly James managed to work his fingers down to the handle and yank it free. With one fluid motion he plunged it into Adam's back.

Adam screeched with the pain and stumbled backward, then fell to the floor. James didn't think—he just picked up another knife that had fallen near him. He crawled over to Adam and plunged the knife through his shoulder, pinning him to the wood floor. Adam writhed and screamed, but he couldn't move. James took up another knife and another, thrusting them through Adam's flesh and into the floor, **rendering** him motionless.

Scrambling, James reached for another weapon—an ancient battle-ax. He wrapped his hands around it and stood over Adam, ready to land the final blow to his neck. . . .

"What are you doing?" someone screamed behind him.

James turned to see Susan standing in the doorway with a small duffel bag. "What are you doing?" she screamed again, clearly **overwrought.** She flew at him, grabbing the ax out of his hand. James didn't protest.

"Vampires never kill other vampires!" Susan shouted. "An immortal life is worth more than a mortal one, James. If a human life is precious, think about the value of a vampire!"

vigilantly: carefully or warily

rendering: leaving or causing to be

overwrought: emotional or overexcited

"I'm sorry." James shook his head. James didn't **refute** this logic. He was too confused to form a decent argument.

But Susan was **implacable.** "Sorry?" she screamed. "You're sorry!" She ran her hands through her hair, and her voice dropped. "You come in here . . . and you do things. . . . You refuse to kill humans, but you attack one of our own. . . . You raise questions that I haven't thought about in years. And I was starting to believe you. But now I see you for what you are—a **liability.** You're dangerous, James. You confuse people. You confused me." Susan turned and fell to her knees beside Adam. She brushed his hair away from his forehead as he looked up at her, **agony** stamped across his face. "But I'm not confused anymore," she whispered. She yanked the weaponry from Adam's flesh, but he still didn't move.

James blinked and looked around. For the first time he noticed that the girls were still there, cowering in the corner.

"It's the last night of the lunar phase," Susan said, looking fiercely at James. "Adam has to feed."

She walked over to the twins and touched one gently on the shoulder. The girl instantly relaxed in Susan's presence, rehypnotized by her vampire aura, James supposed. Susan took the girl by the hand and led her toward Adam. Then Susan pulled the girl's hair away from her neck and sank her teeth into her flesh. As soon as the blood began to flow, she pushed the girl to Adam, who weakly began to feed. Then Susan walked over to the other girl, who looked up at Susan with large, trusting eyes. She didn't seem to realize what was happening to her sister . . . or what was about to happen to her. The girl didn't even let out a murmur of protest as Susan bit down into her vein and fed.

James watched all of this, feeling queasy. He didn't know what to do . . . all he knew was that he couldn't stay here any longer.

But what about Alistair? James wondered, his mind working slowly. *I was supposed to meet him tonight. . . .*

refute: disprove

implacable: unyielding or rigid

liability: burden or danger

agony: pain or suffering

James's eyes flickered to where Adam lay prone on the floor. His wounds had already begun to knit together, and soon there would be no evidence that they had been **adversaries.** But Alistair would find out about it.

And then he'll cast me out, James realized. Susan herself had said that the single **inviolable** rule was that vampires never killed other vampires. And that was what James had tried to do.

James had to accept the fact that whatever a vampire was supposed to be—he didn't live up to it. Alistair could never be his mentor. James was an **aberration.**

With the silence of a vampire he turned and walked out of the mansion. He stepped out into the cool dark night, and he did not look back.

adversaries: enemies or opponents

inviolable: unbreakable

aberration: deviation from normal

PART II

Chapter Seven

Five years later.

James woke to the sound of a strange thud that came from somewhere in the vicinity of his bedside table. He peered at the windows—the cracks around the shades were dark. It was night, at least. With a groan James leaned over and flipped on his dim bedside light and then reached down for the robe he had left on the floor the night before. Two green eyes peered out at him from beneath the bed.

"Solitaire," James said as he reached for the cat, "have you been playing with my socks again?"

Solitaire leapt away, darting for the dark corner beneath the bed with a measure of feline **guile.**

James sighed and stood up to stretch. His body felt good, but his mind felt dull. It was time to start another long night in New York City.

After opening a pouch of food for the cat, James dressed and went out. He had an hour to kill before he had to get to the University of New York, so he decided to walk downtown. It was about forty-five blocks, but the walk would go quickly as James **relished** the sights and sounds, even the smells of New York. Hidden behind his dark sunglasses, he could walk through the chaos without worrying about being noticed. For James the noise and commotion held a strange **serenity.** After he had escaped from England, fleeing from Adam, Susan and Alistair, James was grateful to be **anonymous,** and the masses of people that occupied the city guaranteed he would remain so. James wondered whether he was the only person who found Manhattan **tranquil.** He hadn't heard from Adam, Sus-

guile: cunning or craftiness
relished: enjoyed
serenity: peace or quiet
anonymous: nameless or secret
tranquil: peaceful or calm

an or Alistair in years, and that was how he wanted it to remain. He hadn't heard from his mother, either, and the thought filled him with nothing but relief. As long as she didn't know where he was, none of the others could find him.

Stepping out the front entrance of his Hell's Kitchen apartment, James pointed his feet in the direction of Times Square. He had lived in New York for five years, and he never grew weary of walking through the **boisterous** crowds of pretheater tourists. Their restless energy **catalyzed** him, filling him with the energy he needed to meet the demands of another long, lonely night.

He passed a **caucus** of vendors bent on selling him dinner—spicy gyros; soft, salty pretzels; and sweet honey-roasted nuts. The mayor had declared these men a **blight** on the city, but James disagreed . . . he felt that the vendors added to the flavor of the city, literally as well as **figuratively.** The incandescent lights glowed overhead, gleaming off the reflective surface of James's sunglasses. Times Square was lit up, and James could almost pretend that he was out in the daylight as he walked beneath the brilliant neon.

James passed a newsstand and scanned the headlines. Every paper had it. VAMPIRE KILLER SUCKS CITY DRY, screamed the *New York Post.* CITY **BAFFLED** BY "VAMPIRE KILLER," read the more **demure** headline of *The New York Times.* James bought the *Times* and tucked it under his arm. He wasn't really sure why he bought the paper—after all, he knew what the story would say.

A killer had been stalking the city, draining the blood of his victims with a knife or some other sharp tool and leaving them carefully laid out at the scene of their death. The police had nicknamed the murderer "The Vampire Killer" and were pouring every resource into finding him. But the killer was **flouting** their attempts to find him—each murder was more grisly than the last, and this last had been committed on the steps of the Metropolitan Museum . . . an open space that should have offered several witnesses but didn't.

boisterous: lively or noisy
catalyzed: inspired (to action or activity
caucus: group
blight: stain or blemish
figuratively: in a symbolic sense
baffled: puzzled
demure: modest or dignified
flouting: defying or challenging

James had kept abreast of every **nuance** of the killings . . . the reporting of the crimes fascinated him. It was clear to him that the murders were the work of humans, not vampires—vampires went out of their way to cover up the way they killed, to keep their identities hidden. They would never announce to the world what they had done. But it was so bizarre that a mortal would attempt to mimic the way a vampire killed.

James thought about the many "vampires" he had looked for when he first came to the city. He had hoped to find a mentor, someone like Alistair, who could **nurture** James and help him. He had pored over alternative magazines, placed advertisements, made phone calls, followed up on overheard rumors . . . but each time his hopes had been **foiled.** Every single "vampire" in New York had been nothing but a crackpot. In a city of eight million people, James was utterly alone.

* * * * *

James sat down at the white Formica table in the student union where he always met his new pupils and laid out the paper before him. He liked reading the *Times* because their reporting was **pellucid,** and they didn't feel the need to **embellish** the details of the murder or **denounce** the killer in strongly worded editorials, the way the other papers did. They just let the **grievous** facts speak for themselves. This latest victim was a twenty-one-year-old college senior. The paper showed her photograph—she was beautiful. (The killer always preyed on the young and the beautiful but didn't **discriminate** when it came to gender.) Her throat had been punctured and her blood drained. But otherwise she hadn't been touched, and nothing had been stolen. The police **acceded** that the motives of the killer were **abstruse.** But they felt that it was **implicit,** given the nature of the crimes, that they were dealing with a madman.

nuance: small detail or distinction
nurture: take care of
foiled: blocked or thwarted
pellucid: extremely clear or easy to understand
embellish: exaggerate
denounce: criticize
grievous: terrible
discriminate: play favorites
acceded: agreed or admitted
abstruse: puzzling
implicit: understood or assumed

"Excuse me, are you James Hawk?"

James looked up into the **limpid** gaze of two hazel eyes. The girl standing over him was lovely—café au lait complexion, long, curly dark hair. She smiled at him. "I'm sorry to bother you," she said, "but I'm looking for James Hawk."

"You've found him," James replied. He folded up the paper quickly and tucked it into his book bag. James had changed his last name when he came to New York. Given his past, an alias had seemed like a good idea.

"Victoria Sand," the girl said, extending her hand.

For a moment James was so startled that he didn't bother to **reciprocate.** Instead he just looked at her extended palm and laughed.

Victoria frowned as she slipped into the chair beside James. "What's so funny?" she asked. "You've never seen a handshake before?"

James shook his head. "I'm sorry—it's just that most of my tutorees don't shake hands when we first meet. They just nod at me and say, 'Whassuuuup?'" James added an extra-long American-style drawl on the last word, lengthening his normally clipped British accent, which made Victoria giggle.

"I guess I'm just a little nervous," Victoria admitted. She smiled, flashing white teeth at James, and leaned forward **conspiratorially.** "I just changed my major from English to bio, and I'm still learning my way around the science wing," she confided.

"Why the change?"

Victoria shrugged. "I've always liked science—and I like the idea of doing research that could help people." She looked at him quizzically. "Do you always wear sunglasses indoors?"

James gave her a wry half smile. "Do you always ask personal questions?"

Victoria grimaced, probably worried that she had **transgressed**

limpid: clear or peaceful
reciprocate: respond in return
conspiratorially: sneakily or secretively
transgressed: intruded or gone astray

into some private domain, but James just laughed. "I'm only teasing you," he said. "Yes, I always wear sunglasses. I get . . . headaches. From bright lights. I can take them off, but the light has to be pretty dim."

Victoria nodded sympathetically. "Sometimes I wake up in the middle of the night with horrible headaches," she admitted.

"I'm sorry," James said. "Do you have any idea why you get them?"

Victoria shook her head. "Sometimes I think that they're caused by my dreams. . . . I know that I have intense, **recurrent** dreams, but I usually can't remember them by the time I wake up. Besides," she added with a self-conscious laugh, "I'm usually distracted by the pain of the headaches. They can last for hours."

James wanted to ask Victoria if she could do anything to **mitigate** the pain, but he realized they were getting a little off topic. Which was, he reminded himself, supposed to be Biology 101. Still he wavered, **oscillating** between the desire to talk to this girl and his duty to teach her. James earned money as a tutor at the university, although he really didn't need it. He had inherited a decent trust fund when he turned twenty-one, which his mother had persuaded him to keep in a numbered Swiss bank account. At the time he had just gone along with it even though it seemed kind of weird, and now he was glad that he had. No one could trace the withdrawals to him in New York. And the money was more than enough for one person to live on. Plus James's **innate** business **acumen** had led him to invest some of the money wisely, and it had grown substantially in the past several years.

When James had first come to New York, he had enrolled in UNY's medical program, planning on taking all night courses. But he had learned fast that it was dangerous for him to be around so much human blood . . . it drove him insane. It wasn't hard for him to be near humans as long as he wasn't at Final Phase—but the

recurrent: recurring or repeated
mitigate: ease
oscillating: moving back and forth
innate: natural or instinctive
acumen: expertise or ability

blood itself was overwhelming. So he had switched to studying plant biology, which was interesting, if not that compelling. And he had started taking on work as a tutor in the evenings, mostly so that he would have someone to talk to. A vampire's life was a lonely one.

James flipped open his biology book, and Victoria did the same.

"Whose class did you say you were in?" James asked. He and Victoria had spoken on the phone to set up the meeting, but James couldn't remember all the details.

"Miggins," Victoria replied.

"Oh, right," James said with a chuckle. "Don't sit in the front row," he warned.

"I have never seen a human being produce so much saliva," Victoria agreed. "Doesn't he realize that he's spitting on people?"

"You would think that the people wearing their macintoshes on sunny days would give him a clue."

Victoria grinned. "Macintoshes," she repeated. "So you're from England?"

"Yes," James admitted.

"It's great there," Victoria said with a sigh. "I went with my family a few years ago, and I've been dying to go back."

"Yes, it's nice," James agreed, feeling like a **hypocrite.** The truth was, he never wanted to set foot on British soil again.

"Where in England?" Victoria prompted, so James told her a bit about the old brownstone in London. Sadness crept into his heart as he described the old house . . . and he didn't trust himself to say a word about his mother.

"I just loved the ambience of the place," Victoria said. "It seemed like every alley and every corner was rich with history—this writer lived *here,* this thinker died *there.* The entire place was an **elegy** to the greatness of the British Empire. What I loved most were the cafés and artists along the Thames. It's amazing to have that water cutting right through the middle of the city."

hypocrite: someone who falsely pretends to have certain qualities or beliefs

elegy: funeral poem or song

"Yes," James murmured. He hadn't thought about it, but she was right. He had walked along the Thames often and had always thought of it as his special place, even though he shared it with an entire city. "I miss it," he said, and he realized that it was true.

"A place is more than a place," Victoria said. "Both of my parents say that the places where they grew up shaped who they were. After a while it becomes a part of you."

James nodded. It really did feel like each part of London—from the ancient buildings of Whitehall to the crowded plant markets of Columbia Road to the gilt splendor of the Albert Memorial—was an old friend.

James looked more closely at Victoria. In all of the time that he'd been at UNY, James had held himself apart. He knew people well enough to say hello, and he'd tutored various students, but that was really all. He hadn't really met anyone he wanted to know better. But there was something about Victoria. . . . She was pretty, sure, but something more. . . . She seemed to notice things. And she seemed to care. In a city of cynical people it was a rare quality.

"I've always wanted to visit the places where my parents were born," Victoria went on. "I feel like I would know them so much better."

"I know what you mean," James agreed. He was beginning to feel guilty that they hadn't really covered much biology yet, and he checked his watch to see how much time was left in their hour. "Oh no, I'm sorry," he said, "we're already five minutes past time, and we haven't done a thing!"

"Really?" Victoria cried. She grabbed James's wrist and stared at his watch. "I can't believe it!"

"I'm really sorry," James apologized quickly, silently cursing himself for his **verbosity.** "Here I am, **ostensibly** your tutor, and I'm just jabbering away about myself. Of course, I won't charge you for the session—I don't want you to think that I would **embezzle** from

verbosity: long-windedness **ostensibly:** supposedly **embezzle:** steal my students."

"I wouldn't think that," Victoria said with a smile. "We just got caught up."

"Yes," James agreed. His eyes met hers, and he noticed that her right eye had a small blue fleck near the center of the iris. Beautiful. "I'll tell you what," James said, "there's an exhibit at the Museum of Natural History that covers a lot of the material in the early chapters. It's well laid out and might really help you understand what Miggins is trying to say. Would you like to go? With me?" James added, just in case he hadn't been clear. "I could show you around, explain anything you need help with."

"Would you? That would be great," Victoria said warmly. "Tomorrow—in the afternoon?"

"Can you do the evening?" James asked. "Eight o'clock? They're open late on Thursdays."

"Sure," Victoria said, scribbling down the time in her notebook. She looked up and grinned. "I'll meet you there. It's a date." Then she got up and walked away.

James watched her leave. *It's a date.* He knew she hadn't meant it literally—but still, the words echoed in his mind.

He wrote down the appointment in his pocket calendar.

As if there was a chance he would forget.

* * * * *

James woke up to see the faintest traces of pink light leaking in at the edge of his window. He squeezed shut his eyes and waited for the light to **abate.** Once the room was pitch black, James opened his eyes again and looked around, his head pounding, his stomach churning, his muscles aching. He sat up and quickly lay back again. He felt awful, as though his heart was pumping **noxious** liquid through his veins.

abate: lessen or fade away

noxious: poisonous or harmful

What day was it? James's eyes probed the thick darkness, searching for the calendar, which was obscured by a shadow that lay across the far wall. But James was a nocturnal animal—his sharp eyes had no trouble **discerning** the date. It was the fifteenth. Of course—the day after the new moon. A sudden rush of memories flooded his brain . . . dark, ugly memories from the night before. . . .

James had seen the man in his mind before he saw him on the street. Brilliant flashes of evil intent had torn through James's dreams for two days, and yesterday he woke up, certain that this was the night the man would carry out his nefarious plan. James had seen brown metal and the singular shape of a rabbit's ear. He had heard laughter and then quiet sobbing. The shuffling of a shoe as the man approached a little girl who was standing by herself as darkness fell.

"Where is your mommy?" the man asked the little girl. James heard the voice in his mind. He could tell that the man was trying to remain **impassive,** but the little girl couldn't.

"I don't know," the girl replied. James saw the toys that surrounded her—a ball on the grass, a Frisbee—and the other children on the playground, all of whom were beginning to slowly leave with their nannies. He guessed that she was no more than five.

"Come with me," the man said.

She hesitated a moment, **perplexed.** Maybe her mother had warned her not to talk to strangers? But James couldn't do anything to change what happened next. Despite her racing heart, after a moment she realized that she had no choice, and she took the man's hand. . . .

Then there was a jumble of images and sounds—screams, weeping, pain, fear—a **crescendo** of feelings broke over James as he experienced the child's death. And then once again he heard the shuffle of the **callous** man's shoe as he walked away, thinking, no doubt, of nothing but the next victim.

discerning: making out or seeing
impassive: emotionless
perplexed: confused
crescendo: swelling or increase
callous: coldhearted or unfeeling

James had seen all of this for two days.

Last night James knew that the visions were over. The nebulous dreams had taken shape in his mind, and now it was time to act.

He made no sound as he hurried toward Central Park. New York City was the perfect place to go unnoticed, but James was even less **conspicuous** than most—his **sinuous** movements invisible against the shadowy buildings. He moved quickly, with such speed and **cunning** that even acute human eyes might have failed to see him.

Of course, the sun had already set by the time James reached the verdant lawn across from the park's famously whimsical Alice in Wonderland sculpture. Through the misty darkness he could see the man—tall, slender, slightly stoop shouldered, leading the girl away by the hand. With superhuman speed James stepped in front of them.

James looked deeply into the man's eyes. "Let her go," he commanded.

The man stared **impassively** at James. He smiled, and it sent a chill down James's spine. "She's my daughter," the man said.

"You're a **brazen** liar," James said. "I know what you are."

The man's smile faltered, and slight wrinkles at the corner of his mouth punctured his veneer of calm. "And what if I don't want to let her go?" the man asked. He looked **reverently** down at the girl, as though she was a precious artifact—a treasure that he couldn't bear to lose.

The little girl looked at James uncertainly.

In a flash James had severed the man's hold on the little girl. It happened too quickly for the girl to shriek. She simply stared at the man, who was now on his knees, locked in James's iron arms. The man tried to **extricate** himself, but his **feeble** strength was no match for James.

"Do you see this path?" James asked the girl, who blinked up at him. "Follow it out of the park. You'll come to a busy street with a

conspicuous: noticeable
sinuous: graceful
cunning: skill, sneakiness
impassively: calmly, without emotion
brazen: bold or shameless
reverently: respectfully
extricate: free
feeble: weak

policeman on the corner. Go and tell him your name and that you're lost. He'll help you find your mommy. Do you understand?"

The little girl nodded.

The man struggled to get up, but James held him fast. "Try to move again," James said as he tightened his viselike grip on the man's arm, "and I'll break it." The man stopped **fidgeting.**

"Go now," James said to the girl. "Run until you reach the policeman. Don't talk to anyone else, and don't look back. Go!"

The little girl turned and ran, her light footsteps whispering across the paved path.

The man watched her retreating figure for a moment and then looked up at James.

James's feral eyes gazed down at the man with disgust. The dim glow of the lamplight made James's black hair glow with a hue that was almost blue and made his translucent skin seem **luminous.**

"What are you?" the man whispered. His tone had become **submissive.**

James bent back the man's head, baring his throat. Then he smiled, and his unique visage contorted, revealing his long teeth. "Can't you guess?" James whispered **contemptuously.**

The man's eyes widened in terror, but there was no time to scream as James leaned toward him, sinking his teeth into the soft flesh of the man's neck.

* * * * *

James shivered as he splashed the icy water on his face. He leaned over the sink and stared at himself in the mirror. As usual, the fresh human blood had made him almost drunk, but he was slowly returning to a state of **sobriety.** The cold water, a cup of hot coffee—so much better than English tea for snapping one back to reality—a

fidgeting: squirming
luminous: glowing
submissive: meek or obedient
contemptuously: sneeringly or mockingly
sobriety: clearheadedness

shower, these were the **remedial** gestures that he **cherished**—they returned him to normal and helped him forget his night of **iniquity.** No matter how justified he felt in his killings, in his heart he found his actions as **deplorable** as they were **inevitable.** After all, he had to feed—but he didn't have to like it.

James looked into the depths of his own eyes, wondering if others could read the **chronicle** of his horrible deeds in them. Could others sense his **depravity**? Could they guess about the night five years ago that had started it all?

When he first came to New York, James had been completely **ingenuous.** It was true, he had grown up in London, but he had lived in a safe part of the city and had never had to give much thought about his safety. Even the mugging hadn't taught him much—it had seemed like such a freak occurrence, and James hadn't **chastised** himself much for falling into the men's trap. Maybe that was why he had been so furious when it happened again.

He had only been in New York for a matter of days, and he didn't know his way around very well. Every trip outside of his apartment was part exploration, part **foraging** mission. He needed things—things like shelves, a chair, a desk—but he had no idea where to find them. James had tried a few furniture stores, but everything seemed so cold and antiseptic. He wanted the **antithesis** of the modern furniture—antiques, things with history. Like the stuff his mum had, except not quite *that* old. He had always had a **penchant** for old, comfortable furniture. So he stumbled out every evening to find things, which turned out to be a real challenge since most of the stores were closed, and James wasn't nearly as **adept** as his mother had been at persuading shopkeepers to stay open a while longer. For some reason, the shop owners in New York were **adamant** about their hours. They always **chided** James for arriving so late and told him to come back the next day. In London the shopkeepers had been more **servile,** but James realized the New Yorkers

remedial: corrective
cherished: appreciated
iniquity: sin or evil
deplorable: terrible or shameful
inevitable: unavoidable
chronicle: record or story
depravity: perversion, corruption
ingenuous: innocent
chastised: scolded, disciplined
foraging: hunting or scavenging
antithesis: exact opposite
penchant: fondness or liking
adept: skilled
adamant: stubborn
chided: scolded
servile: acting like a servant
inimical: hostile

didn't need his business, so they didn't care.

But James hadn't given up, and his third night he'd walked out into the **inimical** city to find some furniture. He had taken a circuitous route from his apartment and soon found himself standing before a quaint little shop with a plush-looking wingback chair in the window. The store reminded him of the furniture shops on Tottenham Court Road. Unbelievably, the light was still on. The bell over the door jingled cheerfully as James walked inside.

"We're closed," sang out a voice from the rear of the store. The woman bustled forward, and James smiled at her pink apple cheeks and white hair. She looked more like a country grandmother than an antiques dealer.

"I'm so sorry," James said. He tried hard to look **penitent.** "I'd like to buy that chair in the window."

"It's rather expensive." The woman looked at him **dubiously,** and James flushed slightly under her gaze. In his jeans and sweatshirt he probably seemed like an unlikely customer.

"Cost isn't an issue," James said quickly.

The woman's eyebrows flew up, and James figured she was used to dealing with more **penurious** customers. Sensing that he had her, he pointed to a coffee table and then a rolltop writing desk and chair. In a matter of minutes James had purchased nearly everything he needed, and the woman had agreed that his furniture could be delivered at the end of the week. And yes, an evening delivery was possible.

James walked out of the store, feeling triumphant. It wasn't until he was halfway down the street that he realized that he had wandered into an unfamiliar—and somewhat seedy-looking—neighborhood.

And that was when he walked right into them.

"Where do you think *you're* going, college boy?" the tall one said. His skin was a pallid brown and he glowered down at James with

penitent: apologetic **dubiously:** doubtfully **penurious:** poor or stingy

glittering light brown eyes.

James blinked. *Something about this guy is familiar,* he thought, but he didn't have time to process the thought before he felt a sharp pain at the back of his head. When he turned, he saw that the other man—the squat one—had hit him with the butt end of a pistol. James knew about the pistol without seeing it. "Hand it over," the guy said.

James put his hand to the back of his throbbing head. Images were flashing through his mind. The squat man stepped to the side at the exact moment that James knew he would, and behind him a dark cat padded by. Everything was happening according to some strange choreography—each movement **adhered** to James's mental image of this moment. It was all so familiar . . . the men, the silver minivan parked behind them, even the red light from the neon sign that cast shadows across their faces. . . . And that was when James realized—he had dreamed this. He knew what was going to happen. These two men would rush at him with one **accord,** and they would take his money. And then they would shoot him.

He had seen this moment in dreams for the past two nights and had woken up in a cold sweat each time. Now his dream was coming true. This wasn't the first time they had committed a crime like this, and it wouldn't be the last.

The night in London when he had been robbed tore through James's mind. All of the rage he had felt at his helplessness, all of the humiliation filled his chest. He hated these men.

"I'm warning you," James said slowly. "Turn around and walk away."

The tall one cracked up, exposing yellowed teeth. "You warning us?"

The squat one pulled back the safety on his gun.

Like a bolt of lightning, James struck. He **buffeted** the squat man's arm, knocking the gun away, then leapt onto the tall man's

adhered: supported or tied to

accord: harmony, shared purpose

buffeted: beat or battered

back and yanked back his head. The man flailed wildly as James sank his teeth into the soft flesh of his neck. The tall man let out a horrible gurgle as James drank deeply.

"What the hell—" the squat man said as he struggled to his feet. He started toward James but was **inhibited** by the horrific vision before him.

The tall man's body gave a death rattle, and James tossed him aside, where he crumpled against a brick wall. James stood smiling over the dead body for a moment. He hadn't tasted human blood in over a month, and it was even better than he remembered. His body seemed to be pulsing with life. For a brief moment he wondered why he had ever denounced Adam for taking a life.

There was a short, sharp scuffling sound, and James looked up to see that the squat man was running away. *I'll have to* ***emend*** *that,* James thought coldly.

Of course, the mortal was no match for James's supernatural speed—or his strength. Without thinking, James flew at the man, landing on his back. The man tried to shake him off, but James held him in a viselike grip and wouldn't let go. It only took a few moments for James to drain him completely.

The man fell to the ground, and James staggered backward. He swiped at the blood that was smeared across his face and looked down at the man somberly. James had caused two deaths, yet he felt . . . very good. The blood in his veins was like an **emollient,** soothing him from the inside. He felt calm and clearheaded, but most of all he felt **vindicated.** He had killed, but it had been in self-defense.

And there was something else . . .

Ever since James had come to the city, he'd been having dreams. Vivid nightmares in which people were attacked and sometimes killed. James hadn't paid them much attention, assuming they were anxiety dreams. But now he realized that they might very well be more than that. He'd had hints of psychic powers back in London.

inhibited: stopped or deterred
emend: correct
emollient: something that soothes
vindicated: corrected or justified

Could these dreams be predictions? Clues to the future? And if so, could he act on them? Certainly he had foiled tonight's crime . . . and in his dreams, he hadn't.

Several thoughts whirled through James's mind **simultaneously.** New York was a city of eight million people—many of whom were unquestionably evil. . . . James could predict the future. . . . James needed human blood. . . . James would be **remiss** if he could predict crimes but refused to stop them. . . .

There's no such thing as a merciful vampire. Adam's words echoed in James's mind. But on that night, James realized that he *could* be merciful. There was a way.

All he had to do was find the killers before they killed.

Maybe that was what Alistair had meant. Maybe that was what he was planning to show James when he talked about a way to accomplish "the slay" without hurting anyone who didn't deserve it. "We have the power to choose who lives and who dies," Alistair had said. And James had found a way to choose wisely.

Solitaire jumped up onto the sink, snapping James back into the present. "Hey, there, mate," he said gently as he scooped up the cat and carried him into the living room. Even with the antiques he had bought that evening five years before, his apartment still seemed **sparse.**

James deposited Solitaire on the floor and pulled open his rolltop desk, then rummaged in his bag until he found today's paper. He pulled out a pair of scissors and clipped the article on the Vampire Killer. He scanned it again, shaking his head. It didn't make sense—why would he dream about every other killer in the city except for this one? The Vampire Killer had struck five times, and James had never had a single clue about who the next victim would be. Sighing, James stuck the article into a red folder with all of the others. On top. He liked to keep them in **chronological** order so

simultaneously: at the same time

remiss: careless or negligent

sparse: bare

chronological: arranged in order of time

that he could search them quickly if he suspected he might have a clue. Not that he'd had one yet.

Solitaire leapt up onto the desk and bumped James's arm with his head, demanding to be petted. James scratched the cat behind the ears. "So, what have you been up to?" James asked.

Solitaire looked at him with amber eyes.

"Ah," James said, nodding. "Feeling **taciturn,** are we? Well, then, I'll do the talking. I've met someone. A girl."

Solitaire stretched, then climbed down into James's lap.

"Oh, I know, I'm not supposed to be interested in my students," James went on. "And I'm not—I'm not. It's just . . . she's nice. She could be a friend."

Solitaire blinked up at him solemnly.

"It's true, she is beautiful," James went on. "And very smart. I even asked her to go to the museum with me . . . but that was for *her,* really. There's a lot of useful information in that plant science exhibit." As the words left his mouth, James realized just how much he was looking forward to seeing Victoria again. The feeling almost frightened him. He knew that he shouldn't meet her. He couldn't get close to a mortal . . . it could be dangerous. No—he had to cancel the date. That was the right thing to do. He should tell Victoria to go ahead without him.

But James knew he wasn't going to do that.

James stroked Solitaire's head absently. *A pet isn't the same thing as a friend,* he thought. Something had to break through his **solitude.**

With a quick movement James pulled closed the rolltop desk. Startled at the movement, Solitaire hopped off James's lap, and James stood up.

He had to get ready to go.

taciturn: quiet or distant

solitude: loneliness or isolation

Chapter Eight

"That was amazing," Victoria said, still scribbling madly in her notebook. "I finally feel like I get the rules of genetic **mutation**."

"It's a great exhibit," James agreed. The museum had done a fantastic job **renovating**. The formerly pristine museum space looked like a lush jungle overgrown with plant life that seemed to **transmute** before your very eyes. And the processes were explained clearly and **concisely,** without the **circumlocution** that many other museums employed. Whenever his students were perplexed about plant growth or genetic diseases, James would send them here. Most of them didn't bother to come, though. When it came to science, a surprising number of students were completely **apathetic**—they didn't care whether they understood the material or not, they just wanted James to help them get a good grade. But Victoria was different.

She had paused before each display and read the explanation carefully. Then she had jotted down the **pertinent** points and **adroitly** sketched out what she saw. James noted that her drawings looked like English botanical prints—they were detailed and captured a great deal of information within a few simple lines. Victoria seemed to understand almost immediately what the displays were trying to convey, and James was impressed with her **perspicacity.** He felt vindicated in bringing her here.

James had also been impressed with Victoria's **forbearance.** Whenever she didn't understand something, she carefully studied the **empirical** statements laid out before her, wondering aloud about the studies that had proved them true. Sometimes she asked James for clarification, but usually she puzzled it out on her own.

mutation: inherited change in genetic material
renovating: repairing or modernizing
transmute: change
concisely: briefly or to the point
circumlocution: wordiness
apathetic: uninterested
pertinent: important or relevant
adroitly: skillfully
perspicacity: wisdom or perceptiveness
forbearance: patience
empirical: experimental or factual

James stood nearby, **solicitous** and eager to answer her questions but equally happy to watch Victoria's mind work, to see her hazel eyes scan the displays and to view her quick, **dexterous** hands moving across the clean white pages of her notebook.

"I have to tell you something," James said as they came to the last display.

"What is it?" Victoria asked, blinking up at him with serious eyes.

"I don't think you need a tutor."

"Really?" Victoria seemed surprised.

"Really," James said. He hoped he wouldn't regret telling Victoria this, but he had to—it was the truth. "I'd feel badly about taking your money—you're getting all of this on your own. All you need is a little time and patience to catch up. Of course," he added quickly, "I'd still be happy to help you with something if you got stuck. But that would be more . . ."

"Friend to friend," Victoria finished for him.

"Well, yes."

Victoria flashed him that brilliant smile. "I think I'd rather have a friend than a tutor, anyway."

James smiled back

A comfortable silence settled over them as they stepped out of the exhibition and walked down the wide marble hall. James was quiet, but his mind worked feverishly, trying to come up with a way to **circumvent** Victoria's plans to go home. His heartbeat quickened. He neared the elevator with a feeling of **anxiety, admonishing** himself for not having asked her to meet him at a time that was closer to dinner so that he could have suggested that they grab a bite to eat afterward. But now they were almost out the door, and he would go home to his apartment. . . .

"Are you in a rush to get home?" Victoria asked suddenly.

James's heart stuttered. "No," he said.

solicitous: attentive or concerned
dexterous: flexible
circumvent: get around
anxiety: nervousness
admonishing: scolding or yelling at

Victoria smiled up at him. "Would you like to check out another exhibit with me?"

"Absolutely."

Victoria led James up a flight of stairs and toward the rear of the museum. In a moment James found himself amid a brilliant display of vivid colors. Every object on display was **adorned** in beads or sequins, each **reflecting** brilliant flecks of light, and the effect was dazzling. The World of Haitian Voodoo, a banner read.

Victoria walked over to a section that held several shimmering banners that showed natural figures—fish, insects, hearts—hand-stitched in beads. There was no glass case or anything—the area was **circumscribed** by a velvet rope so you could see the banners from all sides. As she looked up at them, her face glowed with **adulation.** "Aren't they beautiful?" she breathed.

James was more **circumspect** in his appreciation. "Well, yes . . ." he hedged.

Victoria looked at him sharply and lifted her eyebrows. "But?"

James shrugged. He didn't want to **deprecate** something that Victoria clearly found **enthralling,** but the truth was, he found the display somewhat disturbing. It was hard not to imagine the dark motives behind some of these artifacts. Still, he didn't wish to be **pernicious.** "I guess they make me a little uncomfortable," he admitted.

Victoria grinned. "Afraid that some **vindictive** student might grab a voodoo doll from the display and use it against you?" she joked.

James laughed. "Not exactly." The truth was, James simply didn't understand other people's fascination with dark powers. James would have given anything to go back to being normal. He didn't like the occult. As far as he was concerned, the occult had ruined his life.

"It's just art," Victoria said soothingly. "We even have some of

adorned: decorated
reflecting: mirroring
circumscribed: marked off
adulation: admiration
circumspect: cautious or guarded
deprecate: criticize
enthralling: fascinating or gripping
pernicious: harmful or spiteful
vindictive: hurtful or vengeful

these kinds of things in my house. My mom collects these bottles," she said, pointing to a red beaded object. "They're done by a **renowned** Haitian artist she used to know."

"Your mom lived in Haiti?" James asked, picking up on the **inference** in her statement.

Victoria's eyes flickered across a display of two mannequins dressed in feathered headdresses and grass skirts. "She's Haitian," Victoria explained. "And my father is Irish. I guess you could say these things are in my blood."

James nodded and followed Victoria's gaze. He wished that he could see the pieces as innocuous. But he had learned the hard way that evil and darkness really did exist in the world.

"What amazes me most," Victoria went on, "is the way these things are all so **innovative.** I guess some people could argue that they're **derivative** since they all have sequins and beads and bright colors, but you can see that the thoughts behind them are completely original, and the designs are hardly ever repeated." Victoria's voice was hard and passionate, and James didn't think he'd ever seen anyone **emote** so strongly over a display in a museum. The slight flush it brought to her cheeks made her seem even more beautiful.

"Have you ever been to a Wiccan circle?" Victoria asked suddenly.

James blinked, shaken by the question. He shook his head.

"That's what these things remind me of," Victoria said. "I've actually gone to a few lately—my friends Tasha and Nathaniel are really into it. Sometimes I think Tasha believes she's actually **clairvoyant,**" Victoria added **derisively.** "But I love the circles. It's almost like I can sense the **empathy** flowing through the universe." She shook her head. "It's such a **transient** feeling, though, I can never hold on to it for very long." Victoria looked up at James. "Do you ever feel like that?"

"Sometimes," James admitted, thinking about his nocturnal vi-

renowned: famous
inference: suggestion or implication
innovative: original or groundbreaking
derivative: unoriginal or imitative
emote: show emotion
clairvoyant: psychic or mind reading
derisively: scornfully or mockingly
empathy: compassion or understanding
transient: temporary

sion and the way he could see the light that flowed through all things. *The one gift of the vampire,* James **mused.**

"It's a wonderful feeling," Victoria said. "I don't like to talk about it—except with people in the circles. If my parents heard the word *witchcraft,* they'd freak out and lay down an **injunction** that I wasn't allowed to leave the house for the next thirty years. But somehow I felt you would get it." She looked up at him hopefully.

James nodded. "I get it."

They had arrived at the end of the exhibition, and James felt his heartbeat speed up. "Look," he said suddenly, "do you have to be anywhere? Because I think we can just catch the last showing at the planetarium."

"That sounds great," Victoria said warmly.

James felt a burst of elation. She wouldn't agree if she wasn't having as much fun as he was . . . right? It was incredible the way he felt around her. The last person he remembered feeling anything like this for was Patty Griggs, back at school in London. But that was just a crush, and this—somehow, even though he barely knew Victoria, this already seemed like so much more.

He hadn't been to the planetarium since it had been redone, but he knew the design had won **acclaim** in newspapers across the city. As he and Victoria swept through the new building, James had to admit that he was impressed. They stopped in the **penultimate** chamber to watch a general video about space and were then shepherded into the vast domed room.

James sat down in the plush chair next to Victoria. It was a weeknight, so there weren't many people in the planetarium, which was fine with James. He liked the feeling of being alone with Victoria. The lights dimmed and he pulled off his tinted glasses.

Victoria leaned toward him. He could just feel the heat of her shoulder against his arm. "You have beautiful eyes," Victoria whispered. "I've never seen them before."

mused: thought
injunction: command or restriction

acclaim: praise

penultimate: second to last

James looked back at her, nearly dazzled by the brilliant life light emanating from her. She was the most amazing woman in the world, and she was sitting right beside him.

He turned his eyes to the screen, trying to ignore the feelings of **misgiving** that had crept into his stomach. He knew that falling for Victoria was dangerous. And futile.

But—really—what could he do about it?

* * * * *

"Please," the young man said **plaintively.** "Please."

James didn't respond. He stood there, **mute,** as a pulsing beat throbbed in his chest. He felt no sympathy for the good-looking young man—it was almost as if a **gulf** separated him from what was happening. Nothing, not the unnatural **pallor** of the man's skin, not his ice blue eyes, not his golden hair, nothing made James think twice about what he was doing. The murder was completely **premeditated,** and nothing would stop him. . . .

With a coldness that most people would have found horrifying, James began to let the man's blood. James didn't follow his usual quick, painless technique—instead he let the young man feel the pain as the flesh of his neck was torn away. The man staggered backward, stumbling against a garbage can, sending it clattering sideways. But James didn't flinch. James tore again at his neck, then let the blood run down across the blue-tinged skin before he fed. The hot, coppery scent of blood filled his nostrils, and he felt himself grow excited as the young man writhed in agony, held rigid in James's clutches. The thrill worked itself into a crescendo as James fed on the blood and his pain. . . . He knew that no one would catch him. No one could stop him. . . .

James opened his eyes to perfect blackness, **enmeshed** in some sort of fabric. He fought the cloth until he realized he was battling

misgiving: doubt
plaintively: sadly
mute: silent
gulf: empty space or gap
pallor: paleness
premeditated: thought out beforehand
enmeshed: trapped or tangled

his sheets. A small life light bounded up onto his chest. Solitaire.

Taking a deep breath, James fell back against his mattress and blinked into the dark. Even vampire eyes needed a moment to adjust to perfect blackness. He stroked Solitaire absently, trying to process what was going on.

It was a dream, James realized. He had to fight a wave of nausea as he remembered the foul images that had run through his mind. Although James had killed many people over the years—and almost all of them had deserved it—he had never relished the kill. True, he had been intoxicated by the taste of the blood, but that was different. In this dream he had loved the pain.

James had the sudden sense that this dream was about the Vampire Killer.

James thought about what he had seen in the dream. Blue light on the man's skin. A garbage can. Maybe an alley? There had been music—could it have been behind a club? It wasn't much to go on. James recalled dimly that he had caught the outline of buildings around him—all low. Maybe somewhere in Brooklyn or Queens . . .

All he could do was wish that he would have another dream. But it was a tough wish to **muster**—the dream had sickened him.

Still, it was his only hope.

* * * * *

James hurried up the steps to the library, his mind still replaying the dream from less than an hour before. Each moment repeated itself in his mind, the emotions repeating themselves in **appalling** detail, but the images refusing to **coalesce** into a **coherent** whole. There weren't enough clues to go on. Not yet.

James swung open the heavy door and swiped his card key through the security checkpoint, then headed for the elevators. Victoria had agreed to meet him on the fifth floor, on the right side as

muster: bring forth or gather
appalling: horrifying
coalesce: combine
coherent: rational or consistent

he got off the elevator. There were some good study tables near the windows, and she had promised to save them one. As the elevator swept upward, James felt his feet grow heavy. He looked down from the dizzying heights, as amazed as ever at how small the people looked from this aerial view. The elevator stopped and the doors opened, and James's heart began to **palpitate**. He took a few deep breaths, **striving** to **moderate** the beating, but it refused to be **subdued**.

Victoria was exactly where she said she would be. Even beneath the harsh fluorescent lighting, she looked ravishing. Red and gold highlights shone in her dark hair, and her teeth flashed brilliantly as she smiled. But she wasn't smiling at James. No—someone else was seated at the table next to Victoria.

It was a guy—probably another junior, like Victoria. His hair was so pale that it was almost white, and his eyes were a pale blue. James hesitated, staring at them. Bitter bile rose in his throat, and James felt **petulant.** He realized that what he was feeling was jealousy, and he knew that it was a **travesty**—how could he be jealous? But as hard as he tried, he couldn't **forestall** his feelings, and they refused to be **relegated** to a dark corner of his heart. All he could do was try to hide them.

James cleared his throat and stepped toward the pair.

"James!" Victoria cried happily. "I'm so glad you're here!" She nodded at the white-haired guy. "This is Nathaniel, the guy I told you about—the one who's into Wicca."

Nathaniel's eyes landed on James with a coldly **lucid** glance. They swept up and down James's figure **unrepentantly**, surveying him. James had to **stifle** the urge to say something nasty. Instead he settled for a **stern** look.

"It's nice to meet you," James said formally. He knew that his manner was **stilted**, but he couldn't help it—he wanted Nathaniel to leave.

palpitate: throb
striving: trying hard
moderate: control or regulate
subdued: quiet or restrained

petulant: irritable or bad-tempered
travesty: mockery
forestall: prevent or avoid
relegated: sent off

lucid: clear
unrepentantly: shamelessly
stifle: hold back
stern: harsh or serious
stilted: stiff or overly formal

"Same here," Nathaniel replied. He continued to gaze at James with that clear, **straightforward** glance. His features were fine boned and elegant, which gave him a **stately** air. James felt suddenly clumsy and awkward. He wished that he had Nathaniel's smooth, **suave** manner.

"Nathaniel's in bio, too," Victoria went on, oblivious to the awkwardness between her friends. "We're studying for the same test."

"Actually, I'm meeting my study group in the student union in about five minutes," Nathaniel said, checking his watch. "But I wanted to let you know that our next circle will be at my parents' place, up in Westchester, next Saturday." Nathaniel pulled a small yellow piece of paper from his pocket. "Here are the directions. It's not exactly a rural setting," he admitted with a shrug, "but it's the best I could do."

"I can't wait," Victoria said eagerly. "James, you'll come, too, won't you?" she added, looking at him eagerly.

James smiled, although he was racked with **indecision.** The truth was, he wasn't exactly **averse** to going, although he wasn't really **enamored** with the idea of an occult ceremony, either. "Maybe you don't want me barging in . . ," James began.

"We love to include new people," Nathaniel said. "It's always good to get some fresh blood."

"I have to **concur** with that," James replied, biting back a smile.

"You should come," Victoria went on brightly. "I'll find a way to **coerce** you unless you do. It's Mabon—Witches Thanksgiving—you have to be there."

"All right," James said, throwing his hands in the air in mock surrender. "I'll do it." Victoria grinned at him, and he grinned back. Her enthusiasm was infectious. Besides, he couldn't **confine** himself to his apartment every Saturday night, could he?

"Great," Nathaniel said as he swung his book bag over his shoulder. "See you then." He flashed James a smile, which James tried to

straightforward: direct or open
stately: regal or dignified
suave: charming or polished
indecision: uncertainty
averse: opposed or against
enamored: in love with
concur: agree
coerce: tempt or pressure
confine: restrict or imprison

emulate, although he was fairly certain that his expression looked much more **despondent** than Nathaniel's did. James just wished that Nathaniel weren't so good-looking . . . and that Victoria didn't seem to like him so much.

James slid into the chair across from Victoria as Nathaniel retreated to the elevator bank.

"You're going to love this," Victoria promised, reaching for James's hand. She touched his fingers lightly with her own, sending a thrill through his body.

"I'm sure I will," James agreed. He opened his notebook, feeling suddenly stupid. He tried to snap himself out of the **stupor** that her touch had caused but was having trouble concentrating. "Uh . . . there's a book in the stacks I need," he said quickly, pulling his hand away. "Do you mind waiting while I get it?"

"No problem," Victoria said easily, turning back to her notes.

James hurried away, trying to collect his thoughts. He knew that it was a dangerous game he was playing, but he couldn't seem to stop himself. Something made him **cleave** to Victoria's company.

He walked down the narrow aisle of books, skimming the titles absently. When he reached the end of the row, he pulled one off the shelf and flipped through it, then replaced it carefully. He didn't know how long he had to keep up this charade—he just wasn't ready to go back to his seat yet. As his fingers traced along the spines of the ancient books, James had the uncomfortable sensation that someone was staring at him. He looked up and was faced with a **chimera.**

The University of New York library was an enormous building with an open atrium space in the center. The books were set behind glass walls on the outer **periphery,** and as James walked among the stacks, he could see other students and faculty browsing the books on the other side of the building.

And that was where he saw Adam.

emulate: imitate
despondent: miserable or pessimistic
stupor: trance or daze
cleave: stick
chimera: daydream or fantasy
periphery: outside edge

He stood there, immobile, in dark blue jeans and a black leather jacket, his eyes hidden behind dark glasses. And then he grinned.

James blinked, ready to rush the glass, ready to shout, to fight—but in the instant during which his eyes were closed, Adam had disappeared.

James took a deep breath and leaned against the shelf, feeling **desolate.** *What's happening?* he wondered. *First the Vampire Killer dream and now this. Is it real? Has Adam found me—and if so, does that mean that Alistair knows where I am? And my mother?* But James couldn't be sure—his mind had been so overtaxed lately, he could have imagined the vision of Adam. James's body felt **desiccated,** like a hollowed-out husk. Whatever the vision meant—real or not—it wasn't good.

It wasn't good at all.

desolate: unhappy or depressed

desiccated: dried out

Chapter Nine

The ringing phone screamed through the apartment, snapping James out of his nightmare. It had been another dream about the Vampire Killer. He raised a **tremulous** hand to lift the receiver, for the moment still feeling trapped in his dream, wondering if the Vampire Killer might decide to make an **encore** in James's waking mind.

"Hello?" he croaked. The room was pitch black—no light leaked in around the blackout curtains. It was night—he'd overslept.

"James?" Victoria's voice. "Are you sick? I thought you were going to take me to the Wiccan circle tonight."

"I am," he said.

"But you were supposed to be here fifteen minutes ago," Victoria said.

James stared at the clock, grimacing. How long had he slept, anyway? "Sorry, sorry," he said quickly. "I—I must have gotten the time mixed up," he **improvised.** "I'll be there in seven minutes."

"Take ten," Victoria said smoothly. "These guys never start on time, anyway."

James hung up the phone, relieved that Victoria didn't seem angry. Quickly he put on a pair of khaki pants and a soft maroon flannel shirt. He pulled on some shoes, decided to skip the shave, and then ripped open a pouch of cat food and dropped it into Solitaire's bowl. "See you later, mate," he said, giving the cat a pat on the head. Solitaire ignored him—his head was already immersed in his bowl. James smiled, identifying with his cat's seemingly **insatiable** appetite. Active only at night, asleep during the day—sometimes he wondered if his cat was part vampire.

tremulous: shaking
encore: repeat appearance
improvised: made up or ad-libbed
insatiable: greedy or unsatisfiable

James took the elevator to the parking garage below his apartment building and climbed into his Mini Cooper. James drove the small car fast through the avenues.

As he pulled into the crowded city streets toward Victoria's apartment, James struggled to sort his **incoherent** thoughts. He had seen more in his dream this time, and he wanted to remember the **soluble** details before they disappeared.

There had been pulsing lights and short, staccatolike movements. James had been in a large warehouse-style room instead of an alley. He knew somehow that this was a different moment of the crime—an earlier one. The killer had glanced around the room, planning to **despoil** one of its inhabitants. But James could sense the killer's indecision: which one?

The dance floor was crowded with young people—mostly good-looking young men, college age. It was definitely a club. The killer sipped his drink, and James's taste buds registered something strange—sweet and sour, some kind of odd martini. It was completely unfamiliar.

James saw Victoria standing at the curb in front of her building. He pulled to a stop and leaned over to yank open the door for her.

"I'm so sorry I'm late—"

"No big," Victoria said as she climbed into the passenger seat. Her long, curly hair swung over her shoulder as she leaned into the low car. She had on a rose-colored sweater and stone-colored, slim-fitting corduroys. She looked fantastic. "I'm just glad that you're coming," she added, her hazel eyes shining. "This is going to be such a blast. Mabon is the celebration of the equinox, when everything is in balance. It's also a harvest celebration, so there's usually a bunch of great stuff to eat."

James nodded and pulled the car back into traffic, glad to have only Victoria and the road to Westchester to occupy his mind.

For a little while at least.

incoherent: jumbled or confused

soluble: explainable

despoil: ruin, remove everything of value from

* * * * *

"Stop," Victoria commanded, "this is it."

James had realized a few blocks before that Nathaniel's home was probably pretty big, based on the neighborhood, but he was still surprised to see the **colossus** that hulked on the corner before them.

"You can park at the end of the street," Victoria said **placidly.** She didn't seem at all impressed by the enormity of the house.

"Have you been here before?" James asked casually.

Victoria shrugged. "Once," she admitted.

James swallowed the urge to ask her why she had come, whether she and Nathaniel were more than friends, if she was interested in him. *I'm her friend, not the Grand* ***Inquisitor***, James told himself. Besides, he hoped he'd be able to get a handle on things between Victoria and Nathaniel from seeing them together at the circle.

James parked the car at the curb, and the two of them stepped up the front walk. She pressed the doorbell, then walked inside without waiting for anyone to answer the door. James wasn't sure whether Nathaniel would take this move as **insolence,** but he decided to follow Victoria's lead.

The front hall was done in tasteful neutrals, the walls lined with black-and-white photographs in silver frames. James cast his glance across it with an **appraising** eye. The details indicated that the inhabitants had a finely developed **aesthetic** sense—people with taste along with lots of money. Clearly whoever had done the decorating had an **affinity** for simple colors and textures and for furniture with clean lines, things that were **unencumbered** with the sort of **rococo** details that many wealthy Americans seemed to prefer. Still, even though everything was simple, the overall effect was extremely elegant. Stunning, almost. "Nathaniel has a beautiful house," James said, almost in a whisper.

colossus: something very large
placidly: calmly
inquisitor: someone who questions harshly
insolence: rudeness or disrespect
appraising: judging or evaluating
aesthetic: artistic
affinity: liking
unencumbered: free of
rococo: excessively ornate

"It's his parents' house, not his," Victoria corrected.

James gave her a sideways look, unable to hide his admiration. He knew that most girls would have been impressed with a large house—with any display of the **bourgeois** comforts that most people interpreted as happiness **incarnate.** It wasn't that Victoria seemed to **spurn** wealth, but perhaps she knew that money wasn't the most important thing. James was pretty sure Victoria would have still been friends with Nathaniel even if his family was **destitute.**

Victoria led James into a large sitting room, where a **bevy** of students were already milling around, snacking on crackers or drinking beverages from frosted glasses. The instant that Victoria walked into the room, a plump girl wearing a flowing black shirt trimmed with black lace over a long black skirt hurried over and planted a kiss on Victoria's cheek. Her purple lipstick left behind a mark, which the girl wiped away with a finger **bedecked** with four rings.

"I'm so glad you made it!" the plump girl cried. When she smiled, her eyes crinkled up. She seemed genuinely **affable,** and James liked her immediately.

"Tasha, this is James," Victoria said.

"Great to meet you," Tasha said, flashing him a wide, wonderful grin. She grasped Victoria's hands and asked, "Are you guys hungry? There's plenty to eat in the kitchen and way more drinks than we can possible handle, unless we all decide to take a bath in them later."

"Actually, I could use a little something," James admitted. He was feeling suddenly **enervated** from his horrible nightmare and the long drive.

"Me too," Victoria chimed in.

"Follow me," Tasha said, leading them through the sitting room. As they neared the kitchen door, Victoria stopped and said hello to a short African American woman with glasses and her tall, willowy friend. James allowed himself to be introduced, then excused himself. Suddenly his throat felt like cotton. What he really needed, of

bourgeois: middle class
incarnate: in material form
spurn: snub or look down on
destitute: poor
bevy: crowd
bedecked: decorated
affable: friendly or pleasant
enervated: tired or listless

course, was blood, but a glass of water would help.

"Here we go," Tasha said as she walked into the kitchen. "Anything you could ever want and more." Just then the doorbell rang, and Tasha **bustled** off to greet whoever was there.

When James turned, he saw that he wasn't alone. Nathaniel was there, standing with another extremely good-looking guy whom James found vaguely familiar. He guessed he'd seen him around campus. The guy with Nathaniel was wearing a black baseball cap and blue-tinted shades that made it impossible to tell his real eye color. James smiled to himself, thinking of his own tinted lenses. Lucky for James that sunglasses seemed to be in style both inside and out. As James studied Nathaniel and his friend, he became **cognizant** of another dagger of jealousy. *Why are all of the guys in this Wiccan circle so good looking?* he wondered. James had **assumed** that the group would be full of women with a **sophomoric** interest in witchcraft, but it wasn't like that at all. In fact, the circle seemed to be pretty diverse—and the members were milling around with an air of **suppressed** excitement. It seemed that these people took Wicca seriously.

Nathaniel nodded at James, but he didn't interrupt the conversation he was having with the other young man, who was talking about a club he had gone to the week before. James faced a countertop that held a plentitude of snacks and drinks, all of which turned his stomach. He just wanted a glass of water. Nathaniel was standing in front of the sink, but James was **undeterred.**

He grabbed a blue plastic cup from the **plethora** that was stacked beside a large chest filled with ice, **replete** with every imaginable kind of soda and even a few bottled beers. James wondered vaguely whether anyone at the gathering was old enough to drink and decided that it was **plausible** that Nathaniel himself—and maybe a few others—were. James himself was, of course, although he never drank alcohol anymore. It had a violent effect on his body

bustled: hurried
cognizant: aware
assumed: supposed or taken for granted
sophomoric: immature or amateurish
suppressed: restrained or smothered
undeterred: not fazed or discouraged
plethora: large number
replete: filled or full
plausible: possible or believable

and left him feeling miserable for days.

"Do you mind?" James asked, holding up his cup.

Nathaniel looked at him, then hauled himself away from the sink. "You're going for water when we have every other kind of drink on the planet over there in the chest?" he asked.

James didn't know how to reply. He couldn't think of anything to say on the subject of drinking water that wouldn't sound utterly **insipid,** so instead he just leaned over and turned the knob on the faucet.

"So anyway," the guy in the baseball cap went on, "the old place was completely **defunct,** so these new owners have taken it over, and it's amazing. The music is terrific—they have a different DJ every night. And they have the coolest drinks—the grapefruit margarita I had was a banger. . . ."

James smiled to himself. Even after all this time, it was hard for him to get used to **colloquial** expressions in America. In England a "banger" was a sausage. He took a sip of his water, gave Nathaniel a curt nod, and headed for the door.

". . . and my friend got this really weird thing—it was sort of sweet and sour, completely odd. It was a lychee martini—I'd never even heard of it before—"

James paused with his hand on the door. Sweet and sour . . .

"You can't get them anywhere else," the friend went on. "Only at Groove."

"Where did you say this club is?" James asked suddenly.

Nathaniel and his friend stared at James for a moment, then exchanged meaningful looks.

"That drink sounds pretty good," James pressed. "I'd love to try one."

"I'm not sure you'd be comfortable there," Nathaniel's friend said quickly.

James's face burned. For a moment he thought that the guy was

insipid: dull or uninteresting

defunct: no longer functioning

colloquial: informal or everyday

insinuating that he wasn't cool enough to get in. James was furious. He had to know where that club was—he had to. He was about to launch into a **vitriolic** barrage of angry words, but Nathaniel interrupted.

"The club is in Williamsburg," Nathaniel said, his voice appeasing. "Jeremy doesn't mean that they wouldn't let you in," he added quickly, "but I don't think you'd be interested."

Williamsburg. That was in Brooklyn. That fit with his dream—low buildings. But why were Nathaniel and this other guy acting so strange—as though they were **colluding** to hide the club from James? Did Nathaniel want to take Victoria there? Was that it? James frowned and asked, "Why not?"

The question hung in the air for a moment, and Nathaniel gazed at James. His glance was **forthright,** but his face flushed. Suddenly the details of his dreams clicked into place. Almost all of the people in the dream had been men. The truth crashed in on James—the club was a gay club. Nathaniel wasn't interested in Victoria. Nathaniel was gay!

Relief at this realization mixed with excitement over the new information. This was it, then. The scene of tomorrow night's crime. He had never been more sure.

James opened his mouth to say something that would **atone** for his **denseness,** but just then Tasha burst into the kitchen with Victoria at her heels. "It looks like we're all here!" Tasha sang, clapping in excitement. "Let's get started."

Victoria looked up at James and smiled. He smiled back but worried his expression looked slightly **forlorn.** After all, he was thrilled to have discovered the scene of the crime—but he wasn't eager to go and stop it. He never was. But he comforted himself with the thought that once he caught the killer, he would taste human blood again. He desperately needed it.

James followed the crowd outside into the rear yard. The air was

insinuating: implying or suggesting
vitriolic: cruel or spiteful
colluding: plotting or scheming
forthright: direct or up-front
atone: make up or compensate
denseness: stupidity or slowness
forlorn: sad or unhappy

fresh and edged with the sweet scent of newly cut lawn. At the center of the lawn was an altar decorated with pomegranates, gourds, dried Indian corn and a large candle. Next to it was a small pile of taper candles. Each person took one. James lit his from Victoria's flame, noticing how pretty she looked in the candlelight.

The group was silent as the members arranged themselves in a nine-foot-wide circle. Someone placed a pillar candle at the northmost point of the circle, one at the south, one at the east and one at the west. Above, the moon was bright against the inky dark. James took off his tinted glasses. It was a beautiful, warm, Indian summer night. James stood next to Victoria and took her hand, trying to ignore the thrill that ran down his spine as his fingers laced through hers.

"Welcome to our coven," Nathaniel said. "There is a new face among us tonight, as well as many familiar ones. Let us give thanks to the Goddess and the God for this beautiful night and for the balance that exists in all of our lives. Tonight is Mabon. Let us give thanks."

There was a moment of silence, and James bowed his head. He had expected the ceremony of the circle to feel stranger, more **alien,** and he was surprised to discover that he was immediately comfortable in the group that surrounded him. Maybe it was Victoria's hand in his, or Tasha's friendly smile, or having accidentally stumbled onto Nathaniel's secret, but James felt like he knew this group—even the people whose names he hadn't yet learned.

"We will now greet the Goddess and the God," Nathaniel said after a moment.

James wasn't sure what that meant, but then the members of the group joined hands and began to chant. He felt the vibrations of Victoria's voice through her fingertips as he stood in the circle. His chest vibrated lightly with the voices around him, and the rhythm made his body feel **somnolent,** as though he had been hypnotized.

alien: foreign or unfamiliar

Yet his mind was **agitated.** His senses **abounded,** expanding on his already overwhelming vampiric senses.

James thought that he was feeling what Victoria had described—the sense of oneness with the universe pouring through him. But a moment later he was sure that wasn't it at all. Victoria's hand, which was **clasped** in his, suddenly felt like a rugged landscape—every peak and valley contained in the lines of her palm felt enormous, like the chasm of the Grand Canyon.

He looked around, and the life lights of the members seemed to intensify—Tasha's edged with gold, Nathaniel's with red, Victoria's with green. James had never seen these colors in the life lights before—and now he could see them swirling within each person. . . . But before he could think about what this meant, he was distracted by a bird on a bough. His rational mind knew that the bird was twenty feet away, but it seemed impossibly large and as close to James as his own hand. He could see its piercing eyes and even taste the grub it had for dinner. He could feel the energy of its life light pulsing in his own veins.

James's hand tingled, almost as though electricity were passing from Victoria's hand into his own. He felt like a conductor, a lightning rod, throbbing with more energy than he could handle. What was happening to him? Did it have to do with the magic of the circle? Or with Victoria? He didn't know.

James bent his head and squeezed his eyes shut. He didn't want to **betray** what was happening to him, but his senses were overcoming his mind. He could smell the sweet musky odor of the bark on the trees in the next yard; he could see every vein in Nathaniel's face. And the underwater sensation that he had experienced earlier now left him feeling like he was drowning . . .

He let out a low, **bestial** cry, then pitched forward into utter blackness.

somnolent: sleepy
agitated: restless or disturbed
abounded: filled or overloaded
clasped: held or grasped
betray: give away
bestial: inhuman

* * * * *

When James woke up, he was in a posture of complete **repose,** laid out on the couch as though he had fallen asleep watching television. Low voices murmured behind him, and he realized that he was lying comfortably on a velvet couch. He could tell by the diaphanous curtains pulled across the windows that he wasn't in the home of a vampire, but for some reason, the knowledge didn't concern him. Sleep was calling him, ready to seduce him in her soft arms, and he was about to **succumb**. . . .

Then he heard one of the low voices say his name. Victoria's voice. Suddenly the scene from the night before came rushing back, shocking James out of his **complacency**. He was in Nathaniel's living room, far away from his own apartment. *God,* James thought, *what time is it?* He checked his watch—almost 4 AM—less than two hours until daylight. Faced with the sudden, **compelling** need to leave, James struggled to his feet and stumbled toward the voices.

He emerged, blinking, into the brilliant light of the white kitchen.

The low voices went silent.

James squinted and shielded his eyes from the overhead incandescent light. Momentarily blinded, he could just make out that Victoria was sitting at a table with Tasha and Nathaniel. A stabbing pain shot through his forehead, sinking into the rear of his eyes.

"James!" Victoria said when she saw him. She flew out of her chair and pressed something into his hand. "Here are your glasses," she whispered. "I didn't think you should wear them while you were asleep."

James accepted them **diffidently.** "Thank you," he said in a quiet voice, uncomfortable that Victoria was seeing him so vulnerable.

He put on the glasses and felt instantly better as his eyes began to adjust. He could see that there were three mugs steaming with some sort of hot **potables** on the wooden table at the center of the

repose: rest or relaxation
succumb: give in
complacency: lack of concern or worry
compelling: convincing or gripping
diffidently: hesitantly or timidly

room. The room was warm, and James could smell the comforting scent of peppermint and chamomile in the air. He guessed the three friends had been drinking tea. Tasha and Victoria's faces wore concerned expressions, while Nathaniel's expression remained as **enigmatic** as ever.

"Are you all right?" Tasha asked.

"You scared us," Victoria added.

"I did?" James asked.

Victoria nodded. "After you fell, you kept insisting that you were fine, but you were acting really out of it. You said all you needed was to lie down and rest—but I told these guys that if you didn't wake up soon, I'd have to call 911—"

"I'm glad you didn't," James **interjected.**

Victoria blinked, and James winced, realizing that his voice must have sounded rather **brusque.** He didn't want to hurt her feelings—or Nathaniel's and Tasha's either, since they had been so accommodating—but he could just have imagined what would have happened if the paramedics had examined him.

"I'm sorry," James said. "I just mean that I think it wouldn't have been **appropriate.** I'm fine. Really," he added, noting Victoria's dubious look. "I'm really sorry about your circle," he finished sincerely.

"Don't worry about it," Tasha said easily.

Nathaniel gave a shrug, which James interpreted as meaning, "Things happen."

Victoria just kept looking at James quizzically. He bit his lip, **aggrieved** to think that he had ruined their night together. He swore to himself that he would make this up to her—although he couldn't think of anything that would supply a **commensurate** amount of fun to **compensate** for the concern he'd caused her.

But he had other, more pressing concerns at the moment.

"Look, I'm sorry about this, Victoria," James said quickly, "but I have to go."

potables: drinks
enigmatic: mysterious
interjected: interrupted
brusque: gruff or abrupt
appropriate: correct or proper
aggrieved: upset
commensurate: appropriate or matching
compensate: make up for

Victoria shook her head. "It's way too late," she said. "I called my parents hours ago and told them that I'd be spending the night here. You should stay, too, and get home when you're rested."

"I can't wait," James replied urgently.

"Why not?" Victoria asked.

Of course, it wasn't like he could explain the real, hellishly **pragmatic** reason why he had to go. James racked his brain to try to come up with some sort of **trenchant** argument for why he should leave but couldn't think of anything.

"I have to go," James repeated finally. His voice was low and firm—he had decided not to bother with an explanation at all. He knew where it would lead—to an argument in which he would unleash a **polemical** rationale that satisfied no one. And he had to get home. Not only because of the sun, but because of the **didactic** dreams and **portents** he had identified pointing to the next Vampire Killer murder. It would happen that night—he was sure of it—and he needed to rest. He was the only one who could save the victim, and he would not **forsake** him. "It's important."

"It can't wait a couple of hours?" Victoria asked.

"It really can't," James **assured** her. Then, wincing at the **affront** he was about to commit, he added, "I hate to leave you here, and I never would if it wasn't really important." James couldn't be sure, but he thought that he saw a flash of understanding in Victoria's eyes.

"I can get home on the train," Victoria said, waving away his concern.

"You're just going to leave her here?" Nathaniel repeated, his pale eyes wide. He clearly thought this behavior was utterly **reprehensible,** and he couldn't understand why Victoria was being so **pliable.** Although he barely knew Nathaniel, James sensed that he wouldn't have **capitulated** to James's needs so easily.

"It's fine," Victoria assured him.

pragmatic: practical
trenchant: effective or articulate
polemical: controversial or argumentative
didactic: informative
portents: signs or omens
forsake: abandon
assured: promised
affront: insult or offense
reprehensible: wrong or guilty
pliable: flexible or adaptable
capitulated: submitted or gave in

Nathaniel continued to stare at James with a withering glance.

James knew that he had **engendered** Victoria's friend's **enmity,** but there was nothing he could do about it. At least Nathaniel was too **laconic** to **vituperate** him.

"I'll give you a lift tomorrow, Victoria," Tasha put in. "If you don't mind sitting in the world's messiest car."

"That would be great."

"Thank you." James was so grateful for Tasha's **impregnable** wall of good cheer that he could have kissed her.

"I'll walk you out to your car," Victoria volunteered.

James wished Tasha and Nathaniel good night and wondered what the **aggregate** of her warm smile and his indifferent shrug meant. James supposed that he wouldn't be invited to any more circles for a while—which was fine with him—but that he wouldn't be completely blacklisted, either.

The night air had turned chilly. He wasn't sure whether he was just **paranoid** or if the edge of the sky was turning gray. Telling himself not to panic, he turned and faced Victoria.

"I can't tell you how sorry I am—" he started, but she held up her hand.

"I know you wouldn't be doing this unless you had to." Victoria gave him a wry little half smile. "Maybe someday you'll tell me about it."

James didn't know how to respond. Something about her words struck him as impossibly **poignant.**

"You certainly are an **enigma,** James Hawk," Victoria said after a long moment. "Sometimes I wonder if I'll ever get to know you."

"You already know me better than most people," James told her.

That wry little smile didn't leave her lips. "I guess that's true," she replied. "But that still doesn't mean I know you well, does it?" She gave him a quick peck on the lips, then turned and walked into the house.

engendered: provoked
enmity: hostility or ill will
laconic: short or to the point
vituperate: yell at
impregnable: indestructible
aggregate: sum or combination
paranoid: fearful or obsessed
poignant: moving or touching
enigma: mystery

He stood there a moment, listening to the click of the latch as the door closed behind her, before he finally forced himself toward his car.

* * * * *

There is no doubt about it now, James thought as he sped across the George Washington Bridge, *the sun is coming up.* The sight of the sky lightening from gray to pink should have been a beautiful sight, but not to a vampire. As it was, James felt sick. Even tinted windows and dark glasses weren't doing much to moderate the brilliance of the sun's glare, and it hadn't even risen past the horizon yet.

"Come on, come on," James said, cursing under his breath. He wove madly between traffic. He dodged a yellow cab and was nearly sideswiped by an eighteen-wheeler. He tucked neatly between two delivery trucks and burst ahead of them, taking the exit ramp way too fast. James took the E-Z pass lane and didn't slow down or pay the toll. *Let them fine me,* he thought.

James breathed a sigh of relief as he raced down the Upper West Side, suddenly comforted by the shadow of the tall buildings. "Stay down," James commanded the sun.

But the **reprieve** lasted only a moment. As James passed a park, the **insurgent** sun slipped high enough to thrust its rays into his eyes, sharp as daggers.

James screamed—he couldn't see a thing. Horns blared as James cut his wheel to the right and slowed down. He was forced to bow down before the **sovereign** light, and he leaned over as far as he could to escape the piercing glare.

Thinking fast, James flipped the door handle on the passenger side and cracked the door slightly. He couldn't look up, but he could look at the ground. Leaning over, he could see the outline of the cars lined up on the curb at his right. He only had a few blocks to go. . . .

reprieve: break or rest

insurgent: uprising

sovereign: supreme or commanding

Driving as quickly as he dared, James leaned over and watched the edge of the cars crawl past his passenger door as he piloted the Mini forward. A moment later James was back in the shadow of a tall building. He sat up, blinking the stars out of his eyes, and realized that he was only two blocks from his apartment building.

James's hands shook on the wheel as he put his foot on the gas. The light ahead was red, but he didn't dare wait for it. The building beside him was already dark, hulking before the backlight of the dawn, which rose like a **potentate** who refused to be ignored. He sped through the red light. A horn blared as a truck bore down on him. James swerved right and fishtailed, the truck missing him by inches.

The blackness closed in on him from all sides as he drove into the parking lot. He was still trembling as he parked the car. James had never been so grateful for the parking lot's **insular** darkness, but now he felt secure with its weight wrapped around him like a blanket.

Heaving a sigh of relief, James stepped into the elevator and pressed the button for the fifth floor. Then he leaned against the rear wall as the elevator began to rise. He had never felt so weak—it was like his muscles had **atrophied** over the last hour. He was so exhausted that it took him a moment to realize that the elevator had stopped . . . but not at his floor.

With a sickening ding, the elevator stopped at the lobby. In a moment of panic James realized what had happened—someone wanted to get on. He clawed at the door close button, but the elevator doors ignored him, sliding open in their usual **serene** manner.

James squeezed himself against the wall of the elevator behind the keypad as daylight came pouring into the four-foot square. A wide band rained across his forearm, searing his skin, and James yanked it backward. He had to bite his tongue to keep from screaming—the pain was almost more than he could **endure.** A slow-mov-

potentate: monarch or ruler
insular: confined or secluded
atrophied: withered or deteriorated
serene: peaceful
endure: tolerate or bear

ing woman with two miniature poodles boarded in a process that seemed **interminable**.

"Fourteen, please," she said to James.

But James didn't move. His eyes were squeezed shut tight—he had to keep his optic nerve from burning.

The woman sighed and pressed the button for her floor, and after an impossibly long pause the doors closed again.

By the time the elevator drew to a stop at James's floor, he could barely force his feet to step off the elevator. His arm was throbbing with pain, and spots danced before his eyes. Even the dim light from the chandelier in the hallway felt like torture.

James's hand was trembling so badly that he could hardly fit his key into the lock. He nearly began to sob as the latch finally gave way and he stumbled into his blissfully dark apartment.

Stupid, stupid, James thought as he staggered to the couch and lay down. *How could I have been so stupid? I never should have gone to Westchester. What if I had been caught in the full sun? What if that had happened and Victoria had been in the car with me?*

James felt the soft pressure of cat paws on his chest, and he reached up to stroke Solitaire's dark fur.

I have to rest, James told himself. He was exhausted from the drive, and the sun, and the mysterious ceremony the night before. James still had no idea what had happened there. It seemed like his vampiric senses had been heightened by the circle somehow. But what did it mean? James had no idea, and he didn't have the energy to think about it. He had to get some sleep.

The Vampire Killer was going to strike that night. And he had to be ready.

* * * * *

interminable: wearisome, drawn out

James's footsteps echoed surreally as he walked down the darkened street of his dream. Of course, they were not really *his* footsteps, as we was inhabiting someone else's body, not in control of its actions but simply along for the ride. He stopped in front of a nondescript, unilluminated dark door. With the peculiar knowledge of the dreamer, he knew this was it. He put his hand against the door and felt the **palpitation** of the music blasting behind it. Cool metal handle. A large man with a shaved head and a soul patch eyed him as he opened the door and walked in. The man nodded, **intimating** that he could go ahead. James stepped past the red velvet curtain and was swallowed by the dark and the music beyond.

The club was cool, despite the bodies **compressed** in an ecstasy of movement on the dance floor. Against the far wall stood two clusters of tables with a narrow **aisle** between them leading to a heavy curtain beneath a glowing red exit sign. The curtain barely managed to **camouflage** the heavy metal fire door, which otherwise would have stood in dark contrast with the rest of the decor. Brown velvet cushions **complemented** the dark wood chairs and tables, while mirrors with ornate gold-gilt frames hung everywhere. Pillar candles in tall holders stood in every corner, and the overall effect reminded James of a cathedral. Still, it struck him as cold and somehow **artificial,** and even if he hadn't had the **prescient** knowledge that this was about to become a murder scene, he would have been uncomfortable there.

James experienced all of this so **vividly** that he had to remind himself that he was in a dream and he needed to collect all of the clues he could.

It took no time for James's eyes to become **acclimated** to the dim light, and he made his way over to the bar. Even as he ordered, he felt the other mind—the mind he was inhabiting in his dream—**calculating** its next move. James began to grow **apprehensive** as his eyes cast a **speculative** glance over the dancing mass of bodies,

palpitation: throb
intimating: indicating or hinting
compressed: packed together
aisle: walkway
camouflage: hide or cover
complemented: matched or balanced
artificial: fake or insincere
prescient: having foresight
vividly: clearly or acutely
acclimated: adjusted
calculating: plotting or planning
apprehensive: worried or nervous
speculative: exploratory

and James realized that he was inside the point of view of a predator, a killer. As usual, he was already attracting a great deal of attention. James wished that he could command himself to look in the mirror so that he might know what the killer looked like, but he was simply along for the ride. At least, judging by the other men's responses to his entrance, it seemed like the killer was attractive.

Sweet and sour. The killer took a sip of his martini as he stood up and began to walk around the edge of the crowd on the dance floor, where the bodies grew more **diffuse.** Handsome young men of every type were moving to the beat of the dance music that blared from the speakers buried in the ceiling. James knew from the newspaper accounts that the Vampire Killer didn't seem to have a **predilection** for any particular physical type of victim—although there had been a **preponderance** of young, good-looking victims, they had varied in height, weight, hair color and of course gender. But as the killer stalked the dance floor, James had the sense that the man's choice of victim wouldn't be simply **arbitrary.** There would be some strange logic to it.

James watched a hundred pairs of eyes follow the killer's movements. It seemed like any man there would have agreed to leave with the killer if he had asked. James felt a sensation of hopeless weariness, even **ennui**, begin to flow through the killer's mind. . . . He had been through this all before, and part of him was growing tired of the hunt. But the weariness left him the minute his eyes locked on a pair of pale blue ones at the edge of the dance floor.

Suddenly James's heart was racing as he felt his host's excitement rise. This was the one. The young man with the blue eyes stepped forward, and the killer's desire became almost **palpable.** The killer smiled and flicked his eyes toward the exit sign. The young man with the ice eyes nodded, **compliant,** and followed the killer out the door. There was something familiar about him, but James couldn't place it.

diffuse: spread out
predilection: preference or liking
preponderance: majority
arbitrary: random
ennui: boredom
palpable: physical or solid
compliant: obedient or agreeing

James wished desperately that he could think of some **dilatory** strategy. Remembering the agony that the murder **entailed** for the victim, he wasn't sure that he had the **fortitude** to experience it again. Yet his own feelings were compounded with those of the killer. Even as he **reproached** himself, he found himself feeling seduced by **reprobate** desires. The need for power . . . the lust for the kill. The desire to hold this life in his very hand and to take it—this was what the killer wanted and what James, by extension, wanted, too. Even though he had no control of this body's actions, he felt **complicit** in the murder that he knew he was about to commit.

Outside, the killer whispered flattery and **compliments** into his victim's ear, but the young man didn't seem to hear. It was clear that he was hypnotized by the killer's presence. James's heart filled with **despair** as the killer traced his finger along the young man's neck. And then a long, razor-sharp fingernail plunged into the jugular vein.

The young man let out a short cry, but the killer **bludgeoned** his trachea with a powerful fist, crushing it and cutting off his supply of oxygen.

Blood poured from the wound in the vein, and the killer licked it, tasting its salty warmth. James wondered how the murderer didn't seem to feel even a **modicum** of pity for his victim, he just went on **blithely** drinking the blood, lapping at it, **savoring** it as the young man flailed. But the victim's struggle only increased the murderer's appetite, and his excitement grew as the victim writhed and pushed feebly against him finally going limp.

A moment later James felt the killer running.

The killer's feet hit the pavement with almost supernatural speed as he tore away from the club. Down some stairs and into a **subterranean** tunnel. A rush of noise, confusion—a subway pulled into the station, and the killer got on.

From within the killer's body, James looked around, trying to

dilatory: meant to delay or slow down
entailed: meant or involved
fortitude: strength
reproached: criticized
reprobate: immoral or corrupt
complicit: associated with or involved in
compliments: kind or flattering words
despair: depression or hopelessness
bludgeoned: struck
modicum: small amount
blithely: casually
savoring: enjoying
subterranean: belowground

make a comprehensive analysis of the details around him. A gray circle on the wall of the subway car—he was on the L train. A moment later the train chugged into the open air and then over a bridge. He had been on the second stop in Brooklyn.

The moments flickered by, and soon James found himself exiting the train and then stepping into the open air. Then he was running, his feet flashing across pavement. A canopy, an elevator button, and the killer staggered into a hall. He looked up and saw an ancient, dim chandelier casting strange shadows across a dust gray carpet. . . .

And then it was over.

James sat up. He was still wearing his clothes from that morning, still stretched out on the couch, but something was wrong—very wrong. He glanced over at the door, where a sliver of dim light fell across the floor. James walked over to it and pushed gently against its weight with one finger. It swung wide, revealing the hallway's dust gray carpet. His pulse quickened. Had he left the door open that morning? He couldn't remember.

Suddenly he caught a quick movement out of the corner of his eye, but when James looked up, he saw nothing but the ancient chandelier casting its dim shadows.

It was the same one from his dream.

A chill ran down his spine as he wondered what this vision **presaged.** Would the killer come for him? Could he be here now? James wondered. Or had that part of the dream been **spurious**—nothing but a confused recollection from this morning's narrow escape?

James cast another glance down the hall but saw nothing. Then he checked his watch and gasped—it was past midnight. So late.

He just hoped that it wasn't *too* late.

presaged: foretold **spurious:** fake or phony

Chapter Ten

Somber faces stood **sentinel** as the dark, limp bag was wheeled toward the ambulance. The crowd that had been dancing wildly only moments before had turned **sedate** as the moment the police arrived, and the young men practically spilled out of the club to see what had happened. Blue and red lights flickered against the sides of nearby buildings as van after van pulled up and television crews poured out, ready to cover the latest murder. The body was DOA. The Vampire Killer had struck again.

And James had arrived too late to stop it.

James scanned the crowd, hoping to catch a clue or a glimpse of a likely face, but it was no use. He knew that the killer had run the moment he had committed his crime. His mind was too quick and **agile** to allow him to get caught this easily. As for clues . . .

"I'll tell you something," a heavyset Asian policeman said to his partner, "this is the cleanest murder scene I've ever been at."

Just then the EMTs passed by with the gurney. They hadn't zipped up the body bag fully, and James caught a flash of fine features and immediately recognized the still-open ice blue eyes. There was something even more familiar about the face, something beyond his dream. . . . It was like he knew this guy, but James couldn't place how.

"It's like the killer is inhuman," the other cop said. "He doesn't make mistakes. He doesn't leave clues."

James sighed and turned away, knowing that there was nothing left for him to do. Still—something nagged at him. It wasn't possible to leave no clues—none at all. Even the fact that there were none seemed in itself to be a clue.

somber: serious or solemn
sentinel: on guard
sedate: unruffled
agile: swift or alert

Is it possible, James wondered, *that the killer really is a vampire?*

Until that moment James had assumed the killer was psychotic, imitating vampire murders. A real vampire disguised his kill, so that when the victim was found it was almost always assumed that he or she had died of heart failure, not blood loss. But the Vampire Killer advertised the fact that he drained his victims' blood—he wanted everyone to see the deaths and think *vampire.* More and more, it seemed like James was really dealing with someone supernatural—the vividness of the dreams, the cunning, the speed of the murderer. Somehow it all seemed more than a mortal's capabilities.

After five years of being the only vampire in New York, James was beginning to think that he wasn't alone after all. . . .

* * * * *

James stood looking up at the recently **refurbished** facade of the University of New York's science building. It was seven minutes to seven, and he knew that Victoria was inside, in her plant biology and **botany** class. He could just imagine her face—the small tuck that formed between her dark eyebrows when she was concentrating hard, the way her hazel eyes lit up with the fierce light of understanding when she grasped something new as she scribbled **diligently** in her notebook. It had been five days since he had spoken with her.

It had been a struggle for James not to **inundate** her with phone calls after she hadn't returned the first one. He had told himself that he should be happy that she had lost interest in him—he was a vampire, for God's sake. He couldn't love her. Vampires had to be **disaffected.** If they fell too much in love with the mortal world, they could never survive. *Besides,* James told himself, *look at the way you treated her—running off and leaving her in Westchester. What did you expect?* It had been **presumptuous** to call her after that. Yet . . .

refurbished: restored or renovated
botany: plant science
diligently: thoroughly or industriously
inundate: overwhelm
disaffected: discontented or rebellious
presumptuous: arrogant or presuming

Yet he couldn't help it. She had hardly cast a **reproving** glance in his direction the night that he had left her behind, and in his heart he had hoped that she would be able to forgive him.

But five days and four phone messages later, he still hadn't heard from her. So here he was, **dawdling** past her class building in a **blatant** attempt to see her in person. When he had talked himself into coming down, he had half convinced himself that he would be able to make running into Victoria seem like a **fortuitous** accident, but now that he was here, he realized how absurd it was, and he decided to abandon it. He didn't want to have to **concoct** a wild story about what he was doing in the neighborhood. He just wanted to see Victoria. And if she **shunned** him, well, then, she shunned him.

He was hoping she wouldn't. He found himself missing her. It had been better when he had no friends at all—he had almost managed to forget how lonely he was.

The bells of a nearby cathedral began to chime, sending a **dirge**-like song ringing through the neighborhood. Seven o'clock. Class dismissed.

James pictured Victoria gathering her books, scooping them into a pile and hugging them against her chest. He pictured her walking down the long corridor, pushing open the door. . . .

But there were only meaningless faces streaming out from the building. He tried to **modulate** the beating of his heart by telling himself that it would be best if Victoria didn't want anything to do with him, but it wasn't working too well.

Suddenly, a familiar voice called to him. "James!" It was Victoria.

James's heart skipped a beat as he watched her curls bob and dance as she ran toward him. The look on her face **allayed** his fears.

"I'm so happy you're here," Victoria said, wrapping him in a warm hug. "I was worried that when I couldn't return your calls . . ." Her voice trailed off.

reproving: disapproving
dawdling: hanging around
blatant: obvious or shameless
fortuitous: lucky
concoct: make up
shunned: rejected
dirge: funeral song
modulate: control or regulate
allayed: put to rest
diminutive: tiny

James felt her **diminutive** body in his arms as she hugged him tight. James couldn't help sighing with relief at what seemed to be an **authentic** show of emotion.

"I missed you," James said, doing his best to disguise the **tremor** in his voice.

"I missed you too," Victoria replied. She pulled out of the hug and smiled at him. But it was a sad smile, one that managed to **convey** a mixture of emotions. "I've been busy . . . with Nathaniel . . . ," she said, dropping her voice.

A prickle of fear stabbed into James's heart. *Was I wrong about Nathaniel?* he wondered. He had to **concede** that it was possible. . . . He had just assumed that Nathaniel was gay.

"He's been a mess ever since Jeremy was killed."

James shook his head in confusion. "What?"

Victoria's eyes widened. "I—I'm sorry," she stammered. "I figured you heard. You remember Jeremy? From the circle? He was the Vampire Killer's latest victim. . . ."

James's mind flashed on the face in the body bag that had passed by him the night of the murder. It had seemed familiar at the time, and now he knew why. Jeremy. He was the guy from the Wiccan circle—the one in the kitchen who had told Nathaniel about Groove. In his dream James had paid attention to the victim's bright blue eyes and blond hair—but at the circle Jeremy had been wearing tinted specs and a baseball cap. And after the killing James had been too disoriented from his drive and too focused on the killer to place the body that had rolled by on the gurney. James was **aghast**. He felt horrible for Nathaniel . . . but there was something else. Suddenly this murder seemed a little too close to home. . . .

"We were all at the memorial service yesterday," Victoria went on, "Tasha, Nathaniel, and I." Her eyes filled with tears. "It was just so sad . . . and Jeremy's family wouldn't even let Nathaniel speak. . . ."

authentic: genuine
tremor: tremble or quiver
convey: get across
concede: admit
aghast: shocked or stunned

Just then Nathaniel and Tasha walked out of the science building. Victoria swiped at her eyes.

"Hey, James," Tasha said.

James nodded at her. "Hi." He decided to avoid any **pretense** of ignorance about Jeremy's death. "Nathaniel, Victoria just told me about Jeremy. I want to offer my condolences. . . ."

Nathaniel looked at James with a burning glance. For a paranoid moment James thought that he was about to **allege** that James had been behind the murder. But then the moment passed. "Thank you," Nathaniel said simply. But the pain in his eyes was apparent.

James felt **abashed** and wished there was something he could say that wouldn't sound **trite.**

"James was just about to walk me home," Victoria said suddenly. "Do you guys want to come over?"

Tasha shrugged. "Can't. I'm so behind in this plant bio class, I'm going to flunk the final unless I do some serious reading.

"Nathaniel?" Victoria asked hopefully.

Nathaniel shook his head. "Some other time," he said. His blue gaze flickered to James's face, and then he walked away.

"Don't take that personally," Tasha told James in a low voice. "He isn't himself."

James nodded to show that he didn't feel **slighted.** "I completely understand."

"Have fun walking." Tasha gave them a small wave and walked off.

"*Can* you walk me home?" Victoria looked up at him.

No, James thought as he looked down into the **arboreal** green-and-yellow depths of her hazel eyes. *No, I should say no,* he told himself. *I just came by to make sure that Victoria was okay. But if I go with her now, it will be the start of something more, and that just isn't possible. . . .*

Victoria blinked up at him, waiting for an answer.

pretense: outward show
allege: claim

abashed: embarrassed or ashamed
trite: corny or clichéd

slighted: insulted
arboreal: treelike

"Yes," James said. "Of course."

* * * * *

"I've never known anyone my age who died before," Victoria said as she and James fell into step. "I mean, I didn't know Jeremy well, but I hung out with him sometimes at Circle, and he always seemed really sweet." She sighed and shook her head. "But it's been really devastating for Nathaniel."

"He and Jeremy were close?" James prompted.

"Oh, more than close—," Victoria began, then stopped herself. Her face fell. "Crap," she said.

James smiled. He loved her honesty—as far as he was concerned, it was one of her best **attributes**. "It's okay," he said.

"I hope that I'm not outing anyone . . . ," Victoria hedged, unsure.

"I'd already figured out about Jeremy's **proclivities**," James assured her. "And Nathaniel's."

Victoria blew out a large gust of air. "I guessed as much," she said. "I mean, you're a **sophisticated** guy; I knew you'd figure it out in about five minutes. Jeremy was Nathaniel's boyfriend. His first. He's had a tough time dealing with his sexuality, and Jeremy was pretty much the one who helped him sort it all out. It was the first time in his life that Nathaniel didn't feel lonely, you know? And now Jeremy's gone."

"Yeah," James said. He knew all about that kind of **privation** and how desperate it could make you feel. James looked at the wall behind Victoria—it was made of **burnished** steel and reflected a blurry image of the two of them as they walked past it. "I'm worried about him," Victoria said. "Tasha says that she doesn't think he should be left alone for any long stretch of time. I know she'll probably go over to his dorm room later to check on him."

attributes: traits
proclivities: tendencies or leanings
sophisticated: classy or experienced
privation: misery or deprivation
burnished: polished
probity: goodness

"She's probably right," James admitted. He was impressed by Tasha's **probity**—and grateful that she was thoughtful enough to worry about and care for her friend. "It isn't easy to lose someone," he said absently.

"You say that like someone who knows." Victoria's voice was gentle.

James nodded. For a moment he hated himself for **instigating** this topic, but he couldn't back off now. "My father . . . ," he began. He was **astounded** by the almost physical force of the pain creeping into his chest. It was an ancient, **primeval** feeling, one that went to the core. He shut his eyes.

"I'm sorry," Victoria whispered in a **conciliatory** voice. Then more loudly, "You don't have to talk about it."

"No, it's all right," James said, opening his eyes again. He cleared his throat. "It happened a long time ago. I hardly remember him. Just . . ."

"Just what?"

"Just flashes. A deep voice, reading me a story at night. Then he would tuck me in." James was surprised by his own words. He hadn't thought about his father in years, and these were memories he hadn't even realized he had. "I always felt safe with him around," James finished.

"And your mother?" Victoria asked.

"We're . . ." James hesitated, wondering how to put it. "Estranged," he said finally.

"That's too bad." Victoria looked down at her shoes. "Do you think you'll **reconcile**?"

"I doubt it." He knew he had to be **evasive**—he couldn't exactly explain the real reasons that he wasn't in touch with her anymore. "We don't agree on certain basic lifestyle choices. My mother is pretty **unorthodox**." He guessed that was the understatement of the millennium.

instigating: provoking
astounded: amazed
primeval: primitive
conciliatory: peacemaking or calming
reconcile: resolve differences
evasive: vague or ambiguous
unorthodox: unusual or untraditional

"Well . . . ," Victoria said slowly. "If there's one thing I've learned from this death, it's that it's important to make the most of your relationships while people are still here."

James nodded. He knew that she was right. This life, every moment of it, was **ephemeral.** It was important to embrace it while one could. After all, he knew a lot about death.

"Here we are," Victoria said suddenly.

James looked up at a green awning that stretched toward a Gothic limestone building.

"Do you want to come up?" Victoria asked. "My parents are at the opera. They won't be home until late and we have about a thousand DVDs—"

"I don't think it's a good idea." It was the hardest thing that James had ever forced himself to say.

"Oh," Victoria said.

James was about to say good night when Victoria asked, "Why haven't you ever kissed me?"

For a moment James was completely speechless.

Victoria smiled. "You're blushing."

He was amazed at her **intrepidity** and didn't have time to think before she leaned forward. . . .

The kiss was overpowering. James felt himself **engulfed** by the essence of her. It was like the night at the Wiccan circle, when he could feel the presence of everything around him moving through his own being. He could feel the movement of her lungs, the rush of air as the breath entered her body. Heat radiated off her skin, and he could hear her heartbeat, feel the gentle pressure of her lips, the smell of her blood. . . .

James's lips traveled from her mouth to her neck. Victoria sighed and arched her back. James opened his jaws. . . .

No. He pulled away suddenly.

"What's wrong?" Victoria asked. Her arms were still wrapped

ephemeral: brief or passing **intrepidity:** daring or fearlessness **engulfed:** surrounded around his neck, but her dark eyebrows were drawn together in concern.

"It's—it's just—I just remembered that I had to be somewhere," James said inanely. Victoria frowned, and he knew that she didn't believe him—but what could he say? That he was a vampire and that he had been about to feed on her? That he had been so carried away by the smell of her blood that he had been ready to kill her? He felt sick. "I have to go," James said quickly. "I'll call you."

"James!" Victoria called, but he didn't turn back.

James's mind reeled as he hurried away. He was **intransigent**—or actually, the situation was. He had no choice . . . he couldn't compromise. *I could have killed her!* he told himself. *I could have* killed *her!*

Bitter bile rose in his throat, and—for the first time in years—James found himself fighting tears.

How can I live like this? he wondered. *Are the rest of my* ***innumerable*** *years going to be nothing but a struggle to control these urges?*

* * * * *

James flipped through the large, dusty book, skimming over the **arcane** language set in **archaic** type. It was an ancient volume—one of many—that he had found in a seemingly untouched section of the library. James sat at a table, propped behind a stack of books on extrasensory perception. So far he had flipped through six of them, but he hadn't found anything that explained how to expand on such powers. In fact, most of the books were **equivocal**, saying that ESP might or might not exist, in this or that form, but no one was certain. There wasn't a single **inviolable** source—not one certain instance of ESP in any of the books. Many of them refused to **disclose** their sources on the grounds that they wanted to protect them, so James had no hope of interviewing the subjects. Still,

intransigent: stubborn or inflexible
innumerable: countless or infinite
arcane: mysterious
archaic: old-fashioned or ancient
equivocal: vague or ambiguous
inviolable: firm
disclose: reveal

James trudged **stoically** ahead, plowing through page after page of text feeling nothing but **discomfited** by all of the information. He had almost ceased looking for ways to expand his powers and moved on to finding any evidence to suggest that he wasn't the only person in the world with this ability. Was it too much to ask for one **reputable** source to confirm that ESP even existed?

Sighing, James flipped another page. He remembered Alistair's study, which was full of volumes on the subject. Of course, Alistair's library was rather **atypical.** Still, James couldn't help wishing that he had remained in touch with Alistair. The old vampire was definitely a strange guy, but it seemed like he would have been a helpful mentor and **confidant** all of these years. He was pretty sure that Alistair could have **alleviated** the sting of his current problem.

The dreams were getting worse. For the past three nights James had dreamed of the Vampire Killer, and each dream was more vivid than the last. Lately he didn't know where his waking life ended and his dream life began. . . . Some nights the dreams felt more real than his life did.

And there was something else. There was something different about these dreams. For years his nightmares had been more informative than disturbing—they were the **forum** in which he gathered information so that he could both feed and deliver justice. But these Vampire Killer dreams were different, and it wasn't until that evening that James had realized why—usually he dreamed from the victim's point of view. He saw everything through their eyes, felt their fear, and used that information to **discern** where and when the crime would take place. But whenever he dreamed a Vampire Killer dream, he saw it through the killer's eyes. It was almost as though he were a **conduit,** a live wire channeling the killer's thoughts and actions. Yet the dreams were useless. They did not **promulgate** any significant clues. Sometimes James even felt as if

stoically: patiently or emotionlessly
discomfited: uncomfortable
reputable: trustworthy
atypical: unusual
confidant: close friend
alleviated: lessened
forum: environment or means
discern: figure out
conduit: pipeline or channel
promulgate: make known, announce

the killer were controlling what he saw and felt, actually exposing James to his **profligate** lifestyle and seducing him with sensual pleasures . . . showing him the joy of the kill. But that wasn't possible, was it?

Maybe it was just wishful thinking, a feeble hope meant to **buttress** James's flagging spirit. Because the truth was, James was beginning to feel a bit like the killer himself. Although he didn't **condone** what the killer did, James couldn't deny that he found the dreams thrilling, and he found the killer's **propensity** for expensive clubs and beautiful young victims as exciting as it was revolting. To make matters worse, his dreams were exhausting, leaving him weak and bleary-eyed. And it was James's **inveterate** habit not to sleep past sundown. Not that getting extra sleep would have helped—no doubt it only would have led to more dreams.

So here he was, desperate to expand on his dreams so that he could **amalgamate** enough clues to catch the killer and bring him to justice once and for all. But he couldn't do that until he could find out where the crime was going to take place. . . .

* * * * *

"Hi."

James looked up and saw that the soft voice belonged to Victoria. He struggled to retain some semblance of **equanimity**, but his heart was pounding wildly.

"Hi," James replied.

Victoria's hazel eyes glanced toward the chair next to his. "You mind?"

"Of course not." James pressed his lips together as Victoria slid into the chair. He half expected her to launch into an **invective**, demanding an explanation for his bizarre behavior three days ago, but she didn't. Instead she just looked confused.

profligate: decadent or extravagant
buttress: strengthen or prop up
condone: forgive or excuse
propensity: liking or fondness
inveterate: confirmed
amalgamate: combine
equanimity: calm or composure
invective: criticism or attack

"I just wanted to know how you were doing," Victoria said.

James shifted in his seat, wondering what to say. He didn't want to be near her, but he couldn't think of any way to push her away without hurting her. The truth was, he was afraid to be near her—afraid of what he might do to her. James remembered the night they kissed, the way he had almost been consumed in a **conflagration** of desire. He knew that if he started to get close to Victoria again, it would undoubtedly repeat. And he just couldn't let that happen.

For years James had kept his bloodlust in check by feeding only on the guilty. It's not like he thought that was the most **meritorious** conduct, but it was certainly better than what Adam did. He didn't want to be like Adam.

He just wished that there were some way that he could let her know. . . .

"Don't you want to talk about it?" Victoria asked.

"I can't."

Victoria frowned. "Why not?" she demanded, her voice rising. "Are you too afraid of getting into an **altercation** in public? Afraid that you'll go beyond the rules of **propriety**? I'm getting sick of your damn British repression!" Tears were welling up in her eyes. "I don't understand you, James," she said, her voice pleading. "Sometimes you're warm and smart and funny and wonderful, and other times it's like you're not even human."

James wished that he could **disavow** what she was saying, but it was even closer to the truth than she could have guessed. "It's just that I—I," he stumbled, looking into her face, and had to glance away. "I need some space, that's all. I can't be in a relationship right now."

"I see." Victoria blinked, and a tear escaped, snaking its way down the curve of her cheek.

James struggled to control the urge to wipe the tear away. "I'm really sorry."

conflagration: fire or blaze
meritorious: good or praiseworthy
altercation: argument
propriety: good manners
disavow: reject or deny

"I'm sorry too." Victoria's voice was a low growl as she leaned forward and added, "I can't believe that you're talking about *needing space*. Sometimes I think I hardly even know you."

"Victoria," James said, pleading, "you don't understand." He couldn't let her go like this—couldn't let her think that he was just being **stingy** with his emotions. He wanted more than anything to be with her—but it was impossible.

"No—I *do* understand," Victoria replied. She seemed enraged rather than **mollified** by his words. "Well, I guess that's it, then." Her chair gave a noisy groan as she shoved it away from the table.

"Wait," James begged, but she had already walked away.

There was nothing left to say.

* * * * *

James stood before the bank of mailboxes, staring down at the white envelope in shock. Usually there was nothing in his mailbox but a bill or two for James Hawk, a bank statement, maybe a letter addressed to Resident. But this one was addressed to James Weston. And he knew the handwriting—it belonged to his mother. How had she found him? Did it mean that the others—Alistair, Adam, Susan—knew where he was? His mind flashed back to the vision of Adam in the library, the vision he'd been sure wasn't real. Could Adam actually be here?

James turned the envelope over and over in his hands, not wanting to open it, not wanting to **relinquish** it. It was definitely from Angelica.

An image of her face—the fine, **fragile** bones, large green eyes, long straight dark hair—rose in his mind, bringing with it a tide of **turbulent** emotions. Mechanically James walked to the elevator and pressed the button for his floor. He didn't see the hallway as he stepped out and put his key in the lock. He wasn't cognizant of

stingy: cheap or tightfisted
mollified: calmed or pacified
relinquish: give up
fragile: delicate, easily breakable
turbulent: chaotic or restless

turning on the light. He stood in the middle of the living room, and the unopened letter fluttered from his hand to the floor.

A wave of **hostility** washed over him, and without thinking, he turned and put his fist through the top of his glass coffee table.

Thick glass flew everywhere, shattering the last shred of James's **restraint.** His mother! She was the one who did this to him—who made him undergo this **transmutation** from human to monster. She made it impossible for him to have a single friend. She took away the potential for love in his life. She made him a danger to everything—everything—even . . .

Victoria's face **loomed** in his mind, and James let out a low moan. Solitaire leapt from his place on the couch as James grabbed one of the enormous cushions and tore it in half. It felt good to destroy something **tangible.** Now he needed more.

James hurtled headlong into the kitchen and yanked open the cabinets, tearing one of the cabinet doors off its hinges. He hauled out everything, stacks of plates, cups and saucers, heavy earthenware mixing bowls—everything crashed against the peach-toned Mexican tile floor. James felt no **remorse** as he rampaged through all his things. He felt nothing—nothing but the need to **wreak** destruction. It was like a **tonic** to his nerves.

He let out a scream and ripped the phone from the wall, then the clock after it. Heaving, he pushed the refrigerator over on its face, and then he stood there, panting, spent.

James never could have explained the **transition,** but just like that, his rage had passed. He leaned against the ruined cabinetry, then sank to the floor and buried his face in his hands, weeping in huge, heaving sobs. He looked around, unable to believe the destruction he had wrought in his own home. Like the killer in his dreams. He had lost control, and he had liked it.

James felt sick.

Solitaire slunk out from behind the wrecked cabinet and stepped

hostility: resentment or ill will
restraint: self-control
transmutation: change
loomed: appeared or rose up
tangible: real or solid
remorse: regret or guilt
wreak: cause
tonic: stimulant or refresher
transition: change

tentatively into James's lap. James petted the black cat absently, still thinking about what he had done. He had prided himself on keeping his vampire nature buried and hidden, but here it was. Inescapable.

The only question was—what was he supposed to do now?

* * * * *

James looked up at the familiar **edifice** and felt his heart give a slight flutter at the sight of it. It was only the student union, a place of no particular **distinction,** except for the fact that James was certain that Victoria would be there.

James had spent the daylight hours lying awake, **pondering** his nature. He was almost amazed at the **distaste** he felt for himself and his desires. It seemed completely **incongruous** that he could so thoroughly **despise** what he was. After all, if he **eschewed** vampire ways, didn't that mean that he wasn't really—in his heart—a true vampire? It was the simple idea that he had **espoused** for years . . . why should he give it up now? And if that was true, didn't it mean that he could, in fact, love Victoria? All right, perhaps he couldn't have a romantic relationship with her—he feared the **consequences** too much. But he could be her friend. He could be near her and see her. Talk to her.

That was what had brought him here. Still, he was racked with **ambivalence.** The **discordant** feelings of ardor and fear fought within him. Ultimately, though, it was **passion** that came out the winner.

James scanned the space. Students were **congregated** in small clusters at white plastic tables. It took a moment for James to spot Victoria. She was usually seated by herself in a corner, but today there was someone else at her table. A guy.

An **avalanche** of feelings swept over James, nearly crushing him

tentatively: cautiously or hesitantly
edifice: building
distinction: note or worth
pondering: thinking or meditating about
distaste: dislike or disgust
despise: hate
incongruous: out of place
eschewed: gave up
espoused: supported or promoted
consequences: costs or outcomes
ambivalence: indecision or uncertainty
discordant: jarring or incompatible
passion: lust or excitement
congregated: gathered
avalanche: landslide

with their weight. For a moment he was too **bewildered** to move or speak. *Am I dreaming?* James wondered, feeling like a **somnambulist** who had just awoken in completely unfamiliar territory. Even in profile, even twenty feet away, James could make out every detail of his all-too-familiar face.

It was Adam.

James had the sense that he was about to do something **irrevocable,** but he was powerless to stop himself. It was almost as though his footsteps were **predetermined**—every step, every move had been written long ago.

He stepped up to the table and cleared his throat.

"James!" Victoria cried, looking up from her book. Her face broke into a smile, then faltered.

James nodded at Victoria, but suddenly it wasn't her he had come to see.

"Hello, James," Adam said, flashing James an **arrogant** smile.

"Adam," James replied. He folded his arms across his chest. "What the hell are you doing here?"

"Wait—," Victoria said, frowning in confusion. "You guys know each other?"

"We go way back," Adam explained.

James scowled at Adam. Here he was—the **archetypal** vampire—vain and **audacious**. His mere presence **confounded** James and enraged him. James lunged at Adam and grabbed him by the shirt collar. "Tell me what you're doing here, you miserable bastard," he growled. He and Adam were nose to nose, but Adam's smile didn't even waver.

"James!" Victoria shouted, standing up. "Let him go."

The union grew quiet as the other students stopped what they were doing to stare.

"Yes, James," Adam said hoarsely, "you might want to show some **discretion.**" Adam flicked his eyes around the student union to re-

bewildered: confused
somnambulist: sleepwalker
irrevocable: final or irreversible
predetermined: fated
arrogant: proud or conceited
archetypal: typical
audacious: recklessly bold
confounded: confused or upset
discretion: good judgment

mind James that they weren't alone.

James glared at Adam for a moment, then let him go, shoving him backward into his chair.

Victoria leaned toward Adam. "Are you all right?" she asked **compassionately.**

Adam brushed her off. "Quite a show of **prowess,** James," he said playfully.

"Leave her alone," James said.

"What the hell?" Victoria cried. "You don't get to decide who I hang out with, James!"

"Victoria," James said patiently, "you don't know this guy—"

"The hell I don't," Victoria replied. "He works at the bookstore with Tasha."

James pressed his lips together, realizing that everything he was saying was only serving to **alienate** Victoria more. He didn't know what he could say that would **enlighten** her.

"Hey," Adam said coolly as he stood up. "No hard feelings, okay?" He reached in his wallet and pulled out a small white card. "Listen, give me a call sometime," he said to James, dropping the card in his front shirt pocket. "We have a lot to catch up on." Then he winked. It took every ounce of restraint that James could muster not to punch him in the mouth.

"It's a little late to make **amends,**" James said darkly.

"We'll see," Adam said blithely. Then he turned to Victoria. "I'm sorry, but I'm afraid I have to leave."

Victoria cast an **ambiguous** glance toward James. Then her glance seemed to frost over. "I'll come with you," she said quickly.

"I'd be delighted," Adam replied. He cast an ugly smile at James as Victoria gathered her things, and then the two walked off together.

James didn't **hinder** them. When Victoria didn't say good-bye, he knew that Adam had effectively **sabotaged** the situation, and James realized that Adam had come all the way here just to invade

compassionately: kindly or caringly
prowess: skill or power
alienate: push away
enlighten: cause to understand
amends: peace or compensation
ambiguous: vague or unclear
hinder: get in the way of
sabotaged: interfered with or disrupted

his life. He wanted James to know that he could get to him whenever he wanted. James felt a flash of fear for Victoria as another, much scarier thought hit him—could Adam be the Vampire Killer?

James froze, his cool skin feeling chillier than ever as he considered the possibility. He had been increasingly convinced that the killer might be an actual vampire, and he knew Adam had it in him. He definitely was depraved enough. And the timing was pretty eerie—he'd first spotted Adam not too long after the vampire killings began.

But would Adam take such a huge risk, all those big, public killings? It didn't really make sense with everything Adam had said about the importance of keeping out of radar. Vampires weren't supposed to draw attention to themselves; that's what Adam and Susan had drilled into his head. So why would Adam come all the way to New York City to get back at James and then take the chance on all those messy, flashy murders?

Deep down, James had always expected Adam to show up again sooner or later, and he had known that Adam would want revenge and that the plot would be sufficiently **conniving.** Getting close to the one person James had started to care about was definitely a good plan. And even if Adam wasn't the Vampire Killer, he was still a vampire and a killer, and Victoria's life was in danger.

But how could James warn Victoria about Adam without telling her things she'd never believe? He had to think of another way to protect her. James continued to watch the two of them leave, his heart aching. The **glacier** that had grown around his heart in Adam's presence seemed to melt, replaced by a painful ache.

He had **alienated** his only friend, and now he would be back to being a **hermit** again.

conniving: scheming or devious

glacier: large mass of ice

alienated: angered, driven away

hermit: loner

Chapter Eleven

James stared blankly at the television screen, **mesmerized** by the flickering images that cut through the otherwise perfect darkness of his apartment. He wasn't really paying attention, just staring ahead blankly, lost in thought. It had been weeks since he had tasted human blood. Instead he had been feeding on rats, which left him feeling **depleted** and barely **ambulatory.** He couldn't feed on humans because his dreams were not providing him with anyone in need of justice. Lately all of his dreams were of the Vampire Killer, the one **culprit** he couldn't seem to catch.

Solitaire hopped onto the arm of the couch and tiptoed into James's lap. James shoved him away . . . not roughly, but firmly. The lack of food made him irritable. He changed the channel, and red police lights flashed on the screen.

"And now for a breaking story," the anchorwoman said, "another murder victim has been found, and it looks like the work of the Vampire Killer—"

James leaned in to listen more carefully.

"The latest victim was found in her apartment at the corner of Forty-first and Columbus," the announcer went on. An image flashed on the screen—a familiar-looking apartment building.

My God, James realized. *That's this building.*

An eerie feeling crept over James. *What does this mean?* he wondered. First the victim who had been at the Wiccan circle the night before his death—and now this. Was it all nothing but a coincidence? Or was it something else?

Just as his mind threatened to turn his thoughts into something **cohesive**, the screen flickered and went blank. The apartment was

mesmerized: captivated or entranced
depleted: tired
ambulatory: walking around
culprit: criminal
cohesive: organized or unified

dark already, so for a moment James thought that it was a problem with his television set. He pressed the power button several times to no avail. James tried the light switch. Nothing.

Weird, James thought. He knew that some of the older, prewar buildings had problems with their circuits, but James's building had been built within the last ten years. It also had a backup generator—these things weren't supposed to happen. James wondered whether the problem was larger than his own building.

Crossing the room, James pulled back the heavy velvet blackout curtains and peered out at the city. It was raining, and it seemed like the whole world had gone black. There was something **disquieting** about the city tonight, an almost **apocalyptic** feeling.

Fighting down panic, James leaned out of the window, trying to catch a glimpse of a passerby. Anyone. He just needed **reassurance** that he wasn't completely alone. But there was no one on the street, which only **aggravated** his anxiety.

Suddenly James caught a movement out of the corner of his eye. He leaned out farther, feeling the water hit his face, but he could see nothing below him.

He had just started to back up inside when he felt his head jerked backward. Someone had grabbed his hair. James let out a shout as whoever—or whatever—it was yanked his head farther back. In a moment James found himself face-to-face with a vampire. The monster had descended from the roof and now hung, suspended, directly outside James's window.

In an instant James took in the alabaster skin, the glittering green eyes. He sucked in his breath—he knew this vampire.

It was himself.

disquieting: disturbing
apocalyptic: like the end of the world
reassurance: encouragement
aggravated: made worse

* * * * *

James started out of bed, his heart pounding. He looked around his bedroom, blinking at his clock's **iridescent** dial, which glowed 4 A.M. It was all a dream—there hadn't been a vampire outside, there hadn't been death in his building. Not yet, anyway. *Or has there?* James wondered.

Rain pattered with gentle taps against his windowsill. James looked over and realized that he had left the window open and rain was streaming in, covering his floor.

The hardwood was cool against the soles of his feet as he padded toward the window. As he shut it, he felt the cobwebs clear from his mind. For days just walking across the floor had seemed **strenuous.** Earlier that night James had followed Victoria to her apartment and had watched her window from across the street. He didn't leave until he was certain that Adam was gone and that Victoria was safely in bed. The emotional strain of watching her had left him exhausted. But now James felt much better, almost as though he had eaten—even though he knew he hadn't. This **discrepancy** wouldn't have been so unnerving if James had an **inkling** about what had caused it.

Reaching for the window, James realized that red lights were flashing outside, illuminating patches of rain. As he looked down, he saw two police cars at the curb. So there had been a murder. But—but he hadn't dreamed this one. Strange. James closed the window and staggered toward his bathroom, where he tripped over a soft, limp shape. He bent down to see what it was, and his fingers met with soft fur. Even in the dim light James's vampire eyes showed him what his mind didn't want to admit—the **inert** form at his feet was Solitaire. The cat was dead.

James let out a cry and dropped the lifeless body, but not quickly enough to avoid seeing the **congealed** flecks of blood at the cat's

iridescent: shimmering
strenuous: exhausting or difficult
discrepancy: difference
inkling: hunch or idea
inert: lifeless or motionless
congealed: solid or curdled

neck. The animal was desiccated—sucked clean.

James shook his head, trying to keep his mind from making the connection . . . but it was too clear. The cat had been killed by a vampire. A vampire had been here, in this apartment. . . .

Automatically James's hand flew to his lips, and his fingertips were instantly coated with something sticky. Something warm. Blood.

No, his mind whispered. But the truth couldn't be **rescinded**—he had killed his cat.

Just then a sliver of light cut across James's floor. His heart felt like it was clamped in an icy fist as he looked up. The front door was slightly ajar . . . it had swung open.

No, James thought, the image of the dim chandelier in the hallway looming in his mind. *No.*

James scrambled to the door and slammed it closed, then rushed to the bathroom, where he cowered in the corner. He pressed his palms flat against his head, but he couldn't **proscribe** the truth, which rose from the murky **morass** of his mind. Of course. Of course.

His dreams of the Vampire Killer were more vivid than reality. He saw the crime from the killer's point of view. And the Vampire Killer was the one person he could never catch. It all added up.

Why didn't I see it before? James wondered. It was so obvious.

The Vampire Killer was him.

rescinded: taken back, changed

proscribe: forbid, suppress

morass: mess or muddle

Chapter Twelve

James woke up drenched in cold sweat.

Where am I? he thought, panic-stricken.

A quick glance around the room reassured him that he was home in his apartment, isolated from anyone he could harm. He fell back against the mattress, trying to remember the past hours. Had there been any new dreams?

No, he realized, letting out a sigh. No dreams. He hoped with his whole being that also meant he hadn't killed again.

James had struggled to stay awake, terrified of slipping away and murdering another innocent victim. It was the only thing he could think of to do. He'd gone over numerous possibilities to stop himself, but he knew his vampire strength would defy any restraints he employed. No lock or bond would hold back the merciless killer James had grown to know in his dreams.

So James had done his best to stay occupied and alert. He'd placed Solitaire in a shoe box, then snuck into the park to bury him. The rain had battered him as he dug the small hole and placed the box gently inside. James had wanted to say a prayer over the lifeless form, but he found that his lips couldn't form the words. *How could an* ***amoral*** *creature like me utter a prayer?* James had thought, **detesting** himself.

When he came home, the blue lights were just beginning to flash through his room—a reminder of the Vampire Killer's latest murder. He'd put on the television, switching from channel to channel for something engrossing enough to hold his attention. But he was weak and hungry, and obviously he'd fallen asleep.

James walked into the kitchen and looked down at Solitaire's

amoral: without morals **detesting:** hating

bowl. The memory of his cat **depressed** him. Although Solitaire was only a cat, and one would think that he didn't warrant such misery and remorse, that was no **consolation.** Solitaire had been James's only friend for five years.

A shudder ran through his body, and James muttered to himself in disbelief:

I killed Solitaire!

He wondered how he could ever have been so naïve as to think he could live in this world without posing a threat to its inhabitants. He had viewed Adam with such **disdain** when all along he himself had been the bigger threat. He had thought that he'd found a way to master his **cravings,** but all he had done was manage to hide them from himself.

He had committed crimes for which he could never atone. James glanced around his apartment. The **domicile** looked no different than it had the night before, but it was wholly changed for him. Now the formerly innocuous forms of books and furniture seemed suddenly **sinister.** His eye fell on the wastebasket in the corner and the small white scraps of paper scattered around it—the pieces of his mother's letter. In an instant James was overcome with **intense** regret, wishing he'd read the letter.

What had that correspondence held? Why had she decided to get in touch with him now? These questions thrust James's mind into **turmoil,** and it was starting to drive him crazy.

Against all forms of **prudence,** James picked up the phone and began to punch in the number he remembered from his childhood.

A distant ring and then a barely **audible** voice. "Hello?"

His mother's voice. James stared at the receiver. His mother. He hadn't seen her in years, yet her voice was utterly familiar, as if he had just spoken to her yesterday. **Faltering,** he sat there, not moving, not speaking. He had called before he had thought, and now he couldn't **consign** himself to any particular plan. He had no idea

depressed: saddened
consolation: relief or comfort
disdain: disrespect or ill will
cravings: hungers or appetites
domicile: dwelling or home
sinister: menacing or creepy
intense: powerful or extreme
turmoil: confusion or chaos
prudence: caution or good sense
audible: capable of being heard
faltering: hesitating
consign: commit

what to say.

"James?" Angelica breathed.

With that, a whole **reservoir** of emotions flooded into James's consciousness. "Yes," he choked, grasping the receiver so hard that he heard the plastic give a dull crack. He loosened his grip and focused his attention on the sound of his mother's voice.

"Are you safe?" she asked.

This question was wholly unexpected, and it held James momentarily **stupefied.** Safe? From what? Surely he was safe from everything but himself. Silence reached across the gulf between them.

"Did you get my letter?" Angelica went on. Her voice held a strange note. Was it concern?

"That's why I called—"

"James," his mother said, cutting him off, "you have to listen to me. You have to accept who you are."

James stared at the phone, **disheartened.** Those had been Adam's exact words to him five years ago. Accept your vampire nature. **Adapt** or die. Vampires need no **mores.** Was this really what his mother had written to say? Was this really what she *believed*?

"What if I don't accept it?" James demanded. "Why did you do this to me?"

"I don't think I realized that you were different—not then." His mother's voice was low and **imploring,** almost a whisper. "I thought that you would welcome the change, as I had—that you would embrace it, **bask** in it. But you never saw the beauty of what you had been given. . . ." Angelica's voice trailed off, and James wondered if she was crying softly.

Suddenly **enveloped** in the warm arms of memory, James grew **pensive.** What his mother said was true. His vampire vision had been a gift in some ways. He recalled the first night that he peered out into the darkness, the wondrous life lights that shone from every living thing. He thought about the joy of moving under the stars,

reservoir: lake
stupefied: dazed or stunned
disheartened: saddened
adapt: get used to
mores: moral beliefs
imploring: pleading
bask: revel or indulge
enveloped: surrounded
pensive: thinking deeply

of sensing their brilliance, of feeling the thrum of life all around him. Mortals moved about with their **simplistic** views of life, but James knew he saw more. He had the luxury of immortality and each of its **constituent** parts—freedom from the fear of death and time to think. It was a gift. But it came at an enormous cost.

As he **ruminated** over all of this, an intense memory flashed in his mind, hitting him with almost sensory recall. The night of the Wiccan Circle, the night he had held Victoria's hand, he had felt the touch of her warm, soft skin, and it had **fostered** a wild sense of superawareness in him. His feelings had become so intense that he had become **mired** in them and had blacked out. He hadn't even remembered waking up and talking to her, telling her he was fine and just needed to rest. Had he been in the same state when he stalked the streets of New York, striking down innocent people as the Vampire Killer?

I could have killed her, James realized, growing **livid.** *I could have killed Victoria and not even known!*

"You never even **appreciated** what I gave you," Angelica said.

"All I know is what you took from me," James said coldly.

The receiver gave only a small click as he hung up the phone.

* * * * *

The usually **teeming** streets had emptied out, but the gaudy lights still flashed above as James walked slowly through the triangle of space that **demarcated** Times Square. It was late—3:15 A.M. But it was still early for James. He had spent the first part of the evening across the street from Victoria's apartment again, and he hadn't left until all of the lights went out at twenty minutes past midnight. But now there were still many hours in which he could replay his mother's **truncated** conversation. It had solved nothing, of course. He couldn't hope to change his nature. He was permanently altered,

simplistic: basic or oversimplified
constituent: component
ruminated: thought over
fostered: promoted or brought forth
mired: caught up
livid: furious
appreciated: valued
teeming: crowded
demarcated: defined or marked out
truncated: cut short

twisted into a hideous shape. Beautiful on the outside, but a monster within. A creature so cunning that he had spent years blind to his own hideous nature.

He had thought that he was a hero, making the streets of New York safe by preying on the predators. He had felt **absolved** of his crimes by his belief in their necessity. But he had been the worst of all.

A slow rage began to creep over James, and he found himself striding faster, leaving the brilliantly lit streets for some other, darker avenues farther west.

He thought about his options. Suicide? The corner of James's mouth turned upward into a wry smile at the hypothetical scenario. It was possible, of course. He had thought of it long ago, when he had first learned of his vampire fate. But he knew in his heart that he could never go through with it. His vampire nature was **tenacious** and clung to life with a shocking ferocity. If a mortal naturally **quailed** before death, an immortal recoiled from it all the more.

Embrace your vampire nature. The **incendiary** words loomed in his mind, unbidden, lighting a flame somewhere deep within him. Adam had spoken them—and his mother had agreed.

No, James thought, pushing the sentence from his mind. *No.*

He looked up, and his eye fell on a teenage girl. She was wearing a short leather skirt and a **provocative** halter top, her makeup done in **tawdry** colors: blue eyelids, cheeks as pink as a china doll, red satin mouth. There were other prostitutes on the street corner, but this girl's youth made her conspicuous. She stood in a puddle of light cast by a streetlamp, looking forlorn and oddly sensuous.

The moment her brown eyes looked into his, James knew that he had her.

Embrace your vampire nature. The words seemed to whisper on the air around him as the girl's high heels clacked toward him across the sidewalk.

absolved: pardoned
tenacious: stubborn or persistent
quailed: shied away
incendiary: anger inspiring
provocative: suggestive or sexy
tawdry: cheap or tasteless

She looked up into James's face. No one would miss her, he realized.

James took her hand and led her down a dark side street, then into a narrow alley behind a **bodega**. She pressed close to him, and he felt the **incessant** beat of her heart. The shiver it sent through him was almost **euphoric** as he felt the heat of her blood, the energy of her life streaming off her in waves. *I could never feel this if I weren't what I am,* James realized. *If I had not become a vampire, this moment—this awareness of the fragility of this girl's life—wouldn't exist.*

The girl reached up and pulled James's face to hers, planting her mouth on his. James kissed her back, an **evanescent** feeling of desire flitting through him, then being swallowed by the greater desire—for life.

Embrace your vampire nature. The words hovered there, enticing him. *And why shouldn't I?* James wondered, tasting the girl's mouth. The blood in her was **aromatic,** and it intoxicated him. *What does right and wrong mean to a vampire?* he wondered.

He slid his lips from her mouth along the bold blue vein that stood out on her neck. *One life,* he thought. What difference would it make if he plucked this prostitute from the world and sent her into the next? Would she even miss her miserable existence?

One worthless life.

She's nothing but a link in the food chain.

James reared back, baring his fangs, ready to plunge them into her tender neck.

At that moment the girl looked up at him. She showed no surprise, no fear. Only sadness. "Please," she whispered. Her voice was **puerile**, begging. "*Please.*"

At that one word all of the desire poured out of James.

He looked at her closely and saw that she was much younger than he had thought—probably no more than sixteen. In an instant

bodega: grocery store
incessant: continual
euphoric: intoxicating
evanescent: transient
aromatic: fragrant
puerile: childish

he saw the whole of this girl's wretched life, and the pathos of it nearly struck him to his knees. This frail girl was begging him for the chance to live. James was dumbfounded by her **resilience**.

How could he kill this creature when all she had was hope?

He wondered what lies she told herself, what plans she made for escape. But he knew that it didn't matter. He couldn't kill this girl simply because she wasn't ready to die.

Disgusted with himself, he flung the girl away from him and ran off into the night.

* * * * *

"James?"

It was the following night, and the vampire blinked at the round-faced girl behind the bookstore counter: wild, dark hair, thick brows, lots of black eyeliner.

"Don't tell me that you've forgotten already," she said, her dark-lipsticked mouth twisting into a wry smile. "I always thought that I made more of an impression than that."

"Tasha," James said, with a smile at her **winsome** manner. He had come to the bookstore looking for Adam. After days of trailing Victoria—shadowing her until she was safely in bed—James had finally decided to confront Adam. He wasn't sure what he'd say or how it would help things, but somehow he felt like facing up to Adam could help him understand how he himself could be capable of such vicious, horrible murders without even knowing he was doing it. He had called the number on the white card Adam had given him, and they'd arranged to meet at the bookstore. But Adam was nowhere in sight. James had wandered around, browsing through titles, hoping that Adam would appear. But instead he had found Tasha.

"None other," Tasha said, her dark eyes twinkling. She grabbed

resilience: hardiness or spirit **winsome:** cheerful, pleasing

his books and started scanning the bar codes on each back cover. "Sartre," she said, clearly amused at his choice. "Wow—and Heidegger. Interesting. What's this? No Immanuel Kant?"

James shrugged. "I'm a fan of the **esoteric.**"

"A fan of the **turgid,**" Tasha corrected, her eyes crinkling into a smile.

James laughed. "That, too." He guessed his choices did seem a little **ponderous.** Still, he was in a pensive mood—he wanted to ponder the large questions of the universe. "Do you always **disparage** the customers' book choices?"

"Only when they deserve it," Tasha replied **flippantly.**

James had to grin. Something about Tasha was so **amiable** that he actually kind of enjoyed her teasing. It was a relief to have someone to talk to. For the past two nights, when he had come home from watching Victoria's flat, he had stayed in his room until he had thought that he would go mad. He'd finally left to get some new books since he'd read everything on his shelves at least twice already. "So—" James said awkwardly, "when is the next Wiccan circle?"

Tasha flinched. "Indefinitely **postponed,**" she admitted. "There was a serious thunderstorm at the last one—it came on like a rocket just as we started the circle. I thought we were going to get hit by lightning." Her dark eyes were serious as she added, "Nathaniel said that he thought it was a bad **omen.** Part of me thinks that he just wanted to stop holding circles at his house. It was too hard, you know, because of Jeremy. The general **consensus** was that we should hold off on the next meeting."

"That sucks," James said.

Tasha laughed.

"What's so funny?" James demanded.

"Nothing, nothing." She shook her head. "That just sounded really funny in your English accent."

esoteric: unusual or little known
turgid: dull
ponderous: extremely dull
disparage: mock or ridicule
flippantly: jokingly or offhandedly
amiable: likable or friendly
postponed: delayed
omen: sign or warning
consensus: agreement

A soft silence settled across the counter between them. *Don't ask about Victoria,* James commanded himself, but the thought only **exacerbated** his desire to say Victoria's name, to hear those four **sublime** syllables. He knew that he should leave before he fell into that trap, but he couldn't make himself move.

"So," Tasha said finally, "how's Victoria?"

James frowned. "You've seen her more recently than I have."

"Really?" Tasha asked. "But I haven't seen her in days. Wow, I should call her."

James felt his eyebrows draw together in an expression of worry. "Wait—," he said, "she hasn't been in class?"

"Nope." Tasha shrugged. "I guess she's sick or something."

"Yes," James said faintly as his heart thundered in his ears. "I'm sure she's just sick." But saying it did nothing to **dispel** his fear. *What has she been doing*? James wondered. "Actually," James said slowly, "I came here looking for Adam Miller. Do you know him?"

"Sure, I know him," Tasha said with another shrug. "But he isn't here. He's supposed to be, though. If you see him, tell him that the manager is pissed." A chill shot down James's spine. Adam had tricked him!

"Hey," Tasha called as James hurried out the door. "You forgot your books!"

But the little bell over the door had already let out a jingle as the door sighed closed.

* * * * *

Victoria didn't look up, even though she must have heard his footsteps crossing the flagstones toward her. She was seated on a bench, her head bowed in an attitude of **morose** contemplation. Still, even with eyes rimmed red and a face blotched with tears, her **pulchritude** was stunning. James's heart thumped in silent grati-

exacerbated: intensified or made worse

sublime: magnificent or inspirational

dispel: dismiss

morose: gloomy or glum

pulchritude: physical beauty

tude to the doorman who had told him where she was and had let him into the courtyard at the rear of the apartment building. She was alive.

James had told himself that he would be **resolute**—that he would turn back the moment he saw her and knew that she was safe. He wouldn't speak to her. He wouldn't touch her or go near her. How could he when there was a monstrous killer in him? But all of his **resolve** evaporated at the sight of her misery. He sat down beside her and traced the track of a tear with a fingertip. "What's wrong?" he whispered.

For a moment she didn't answer. She just leaned her head against his shoulder in silence as the tears streamed down her face. Finally she said, "It's just—it's just everything. My life seems so **fraught** with drama right now. Jeremy's dead. And now there are no more Wiccan circles, and those were the only things that made me feel better, you know?" She looked up at him with her soothing hazel eyes, and James had to fight the **inclination** to lean down and kiss her. Their eyes locked for a moment, and then Victoria said, "And there's you . . ."

James had to look away. "I'm sorry." She would never know how **contrite** he really was. He knew that he was hurting her, but there was nothing he could do about it.

"Me too."

James breathed in the air, slowly and deliberately. He didn't really need to breathe, and so when he did, it was always in order to take in the scents around him. It was fall, and he caught the **pungent** odor of rotting leaves, the soothing smell of wood smoke from someone's chimney and the warm, musky scent of Victoria herself. His senses were heightened, as they had been at the Wiccan circle, only not as intensely. He wished he could live in this moment forever, with his arm around Victoria, breathing in the smell of her hair.

But that could never happen.

resolute: firm or steadfast
resolve: determination
fraught: full or weighed down
inclination: tendency or desire
contrite: sorry or ashamed
pungent: sharp or strong

Victoria wiped at her face and sat up. "I have to go," she said quietly. "I'm meeting someone."

James's heart stumbled. "Adam?" he asked hoarsely.

Victoria looked at him sharply. "Is that a problem?" she asked.

James hesitated, knowing that what he was about to say would be **contentious.** Still, he just couldn't let her go. "Yes," he said. "It's a problem."

Victoria's face clouded over, and her spine went rigid. "What is that supposed to mean?" she demanded. "You don't get to dictate my life. It's one thing if you don't want to see me, but you don't get to waltz in here anytime you feel like it and try to keep me from seeing anyone else."

"It's not anyone else," James insisted. "It's just him. Just him . . . and me." He pressed his lips together, then had to force himself to go on. "You don't understand," he said finally. "We're . . . different." He leaned forward and took off his tinted lenses and then allowed his eyes to lock on hers. He didn't want to **dissemble** anymore. He wanted her to see him as he was. To know what he was. "We're dangerous."

Victoria stared at him for a moment, trying to **ascertain** his meaning. "How?" She spoke in a whisper, as though she was afraid of giving shape to the **amorphous** ideas he spoke about.

James was certain that she didn't want to know the truth, but he couldn't hide it from her anymore. And somehow James felt that if he told her everything, she would understand. She might not be able to forgive him, but at least she would understand. . . .

"I'm not who you think I am," James said at last. "I've done something wrong—"

Just then there was a creak as the rear door of the apartment building opened. Victoria and James looked over the hedge that separated their line of sight from the door at the same moment, and James immediately recognized Adam's **smug** smile. Victoria stood

contentious: touchy or controversial
dissemble: stall or evade
ascertain: find out
amorphous: vague
smug: self-satisfied

up and took a step toward Adam, and with lightning speed James vaulted over the high wall that surrounded the courtyard.

By the time Victoria turned around, he was already gone.

Chapter Thirteen

A thousand arguments, from the **eloquent** to the **convoluted,** whipped through James's mind as he walked down the street. *I should have said anything,* he upbraided himself, *anything to keep her from him.* There were a million arguments and **assertions** he could have thrust at her. But he hadn't dared to get into another physical confrontation with Adam—it only would have alienated Victoria further.

Victoria's head disappeared down a subway stair, and James hurried after her. He wasn't about to let her or Adam out of his sight.

James stood by a newsstand as Victoria and Adam waited on the platform for the Q train to pull into the station. James idly wondered where they could be going as he scanned the news racks. A front page headline screamed at him: vampire killer strikes again!

James pulled the paper from the pile and thrust some change at the vendor, overwhelmed by a mixture of disbelief and a sense of **morbid** curiosity. Another victim? But James hadn't dreamed of this death. And James had been bolted into his apartment every night. It wasn't possible. . . . It wasn't. . . .

He scanned the paper, and his eyes lit on the time of death. 3:15 am the night before. 3:15. But that couldn't be. . . .

James had looked at his watch at three-fifteen. He had been with the prostitute. But he had left her alive.

The victim was a young African American woman, the paper read. James scanned further. *Found in the Bronx.*

African American. The Bronx. The prostitute had been white. . . . James had been near Times Square. . . .

But . . . But . . .

eloquent: persuasive or articulate

convoluted: long-winded

assertions: statements or claims

morbid: dark or gruesome

James's mind faltered under the weight of these **patent incongruities.** It wasn't possible. He couldn't have committed the murder.

But this didn't seem like a copycat—the crime was just like the others, and again, the killer hadn't left a single clue.

Relief washed over James as the tension that had filled his body for days began to subside. It wasn't him—he wasn't the Vampire Killer. But then who was it?

Suddenly James's gaze flicked back to Adam and Victoria, and he blinked, wondering how he could have been so dense.

He'd wondered if Adam could be the killer, but he'd brushed the idea off so easily just because of things Adam had said years ago in London. How could he know how Adam had changed? Or what went on in his maniacal mind? If the goal of the murders was to convince James that he himself was responsible, that put everything in a different light.

No wonder the dreams had been so vivid, so different than the others James had about regular killers. It wasn't because James was the real murderer—it was because it was another vampire.

James shuddered as he imagined Adam stalking him, meeting Victoria, setting James up. . . . *He probably laughed when he killed my cat,* James thought, a bitter taste in his mouth. He imagined Adam standing over him, feeding a trickle of blood to James so that he would think he had committed the crime himself.

James hadn't thought Adam was smart enough for anything like this, but clearly Adam was far more cunning and dangerous than James had ever realized.

With a huffing sigh, the Q train pulled into the station. James shot down the stairs and waited until the crowd on the platform had **dispersed,** then slipped into the last car.

Now that he knew what Adam was really about, he wasn't ever going to stop following him.

patent: obvious **incongruities:** mismatches **dispersed:** scattered

* * * * *

The train **accelerated,** rocking gently, as James thought about Adam's **agenda.** What would be his next move? **Urban** graffiti gave way to tidy little houses as the train chugged deeper into Brooklyn. If Adam just wanted to kill Victoria, he could have done that already. James had been sure from the beginning that Adam was just using Victoria to get to him, and that hadn't changed. But it went deeper than that. Adam was daring him to try to **thwart** him. He wanted James to know that he was feeble compared with him.

James peered through the glass windows that stood between his car and Adam's. James watched, filled with **loathing,** as the **malefactor** smiled at Victoria and touched her hair. *You're going to die,* James thought as he **glowered** at Adam. *I'll kill you for touching her.*

James had **deduced** their destination even before the train pulled to a stop at an amusement park. Of course. No doubt Adam had convinced Victoria that the amusement park would be the perfect **balm** for her **melancholy.** *How thoughtful,* James said to himself bitterly.

Flags, faded and ragged from the summer's **malicious** forces, **billowed** on the late fall breeze above the tops of rides and games. It was still Indian summer and a pleasant fall night, but James hardly noticed this as he followed Adam **stealthily** into the park. The riotous noise, flashing lights and smells, both **putrid** and sweet, **assaulted** James the moment he entered. Adam disappeared for a moment, **befuddling** James, but he managed to spot him again buying ride tickets at a booth. The park was almost deserted, but James had no trouble hiding himself in the shadows as Adam and Victoria boarded the car for the haunted house.

James buttoned up his jacket as the sinister abode swallowed up Adam and Victoria. A **bizarre, disfigured** *papier-mâché* face

accelerated: sped up
agenda: plan or program
urban: city
thwart: put a stop to
loathing: hatred
malefactor: villain or criminal
glowered: looked angrily
deduced: figured out
balm: relief
melancholy: sadness
malicious: nasty or harmful
billowed: fluttered or waved
stealthily: silently or sneakily
putrid: rotten
assaulted: attacked
befuddling: confusing
bizarre: strange
disfigured: deformed

grinned down at James, and he shivered. There was something about the **ambience** of the deserted park at night that sent a chill down his spine and gave him a sense of impending **catastrophe.** He had no idea what he was going to do, but he knew that it would be something drastic.

James pressed himself farther into the darkness as Adam and Victoria exited the ride, laughing. But the quick flash of Adam's eyes told him that he had been seen. Adam grinned contemptuously, but he didn't **beckon** to him or give any other sign of recognition. Apparently he wasn't yet ready to confront James. Adam simply took Victoria's hand and led her away.

Victoria and Adam **meandered** through the **labyrinth** of carnival attractions. Although James was following Adam, it was Victoria he was watching as she passed from one ride to another. Her skin glowed pink, then green, then blue, chameleonlike in the alternating lights.

James moved quickly and quietly behind them, following their footsteps through the maze of rides as closely as he could without attracting attention. Adam led Victoria onto the carousel, and James watched from a distance, their figures **distinct** against the playful colors of the children's ride. They went around once, twice, but on the third rotation, their horses were empty. James started and looked around, finally spotting them walking toward a cotton candy stand. **Exasperated,** James followed them, cursing silently.

He lost them at the game booths. One moment they were there, and the next moment they had disappeared among the **multifarious** distractions. But James **persisted** in tracking them. Losing sight of them was an **obstacle,** but it was one that he could overcome. He sniffed the wind and caught the faintest scent of Victoria. It was coming from the beach.

James hurried toward the boardwalk, then down the stairs. He looked out at the ocean, then along the shore, scanning the horizon

ambience: atmosphere
catastrophe: disaster
beckon: signal or gesture
meandered: wandered or zigzagged
labyrinth: maze
distinct: clear or well defined
exasperated: frustrated or annoyed
multifarious: various
persisted: kept on
obstacle: barrier or difficulty

systematically for any sign of Adam. Nothing.

Suddenly there was a slight gasp from behind him. James turned, facing the boardwalk. No **Access** read a sign posted at the dark edge of the shadows thrown by the wooden overhang. The sigh had come from the direction of the sign.

James edged closer, thanking **providence** for the **seclusion** of their location. He knew that this would be his final stand against Adam, and there would be only one victor. It was kill or be killed—there was simply no **alternative.** And there could be no witnesses. He just hoped that he wasn't too late.

The air seemed thick in the tight space beneath the boardwalk. The rich, coppery scent of blood filled James's nostrils, and through the absolute darkness he caught sight of a fading life light. No, no, it couldn't be. . . . James's heart twisted painfully in his chest, and he had to use every ounce of restraint not to scream at the sight of Adam's lips at Victoria's neck.

In a whirlwind of **frenetic** motion James lunged forward and tore Adam from Victoria. Adam stumbled backward and dropped into the sand under the force of James's blow. Quickly, James rushed to lift Victoria's limp head, which lolled to the side. Her eyes were half–closed, her pulse weak. The sight of her so close to death **ignited** a fierce passion in James—the passion to help her live. His own body contained the **antidote** to her suffering. Without thinking, he sank his teeth into his own wrist and put the bloody vein to her lips.

For an instant James's heart **contracted** as he thought she wouldn't take the blood. He forced the wrist against her lips, fighting the obstacle of her teeth, and a second later she began to draw on it. James's body was flooded with relief. In that moment he didn't think about the existence he was **condemning** Victoria to—he only wanted her to survive.

James bent over her, **unflinching,** as she drank with more inten-

systematically: thoroughly or methodically
access: admittance
providence: divine guidance
seclusion: isolation or privacy
alternative: other choice
frenetic: wild or frantic
ignited: set fire to
antidote: cure
contracted: tightened
condemning: accusing or criticizing
unflinching: persistent

sity. He was surprised that she **evinced** such an immediate desire for the **consumption** of blood—surprised and a little frightened. What had he unleashed? Her desire didn't abate, and after a moment James realized that he couldn't **quench** her thirst—he had barely enough blood to **sustain** his own life, much less hers and his together. He pushed her away from him. Victoria looked up, and her eyes seemed to come into focus.

"James?" she whispered, blinking rapidly. She peered around, shaking her head, and James knew that she was experiencing her new nocturnal vision. Her face was pale—she was clearly still weak.

A low laugh sounded behind him, and James turned to see Adam grinning obscenely. "Quite the bastion of **turpitude** now, aren't you, James?" he mocked.

It was more than James could **tolerate.** "Now it's just you and me," James growled.

Adam nodded **obediently,** then set his legs apart in a wide **stance** and beckoned James forward.

James hurtled at Adam and struck a **devastating** blow against the vampire's chest that sent him reeling backward about ten yards. James staggered from the effort, but Adam stood up a moment later, unhurt. He grinned. "Is that the best you've got?" he snarled. Without waiting for a response he **retaliated,** leaping through the air to strike at James with his foot. The kick to the chest sent James sprawling face-first into the sand. Before he could clear his eyes, James felt a foot strike his back in a **ruthless** blow. Pain shot through his body, momentarily paralyzing him. He twisted away and managed to catch Adam's ankle before the next kick landed. James sent his foot hurtling upward into Adam's stomach, and the vampire flew five feet into the air and landed flat on his back.

But Adam was **indefatigable.** Just as James staggered to his feet, Adam leapt up and flew at him, delivering a **punitive** blow. James heard Victoria scream and felt the sensation of flying as he was

evinced: displayed
consumption: eating or drinking
quench: satisfy
sustain: maintain
turpitude: immorality or baseness
tolerate: put up with
obediently: submissively
stance: posture
devastating: damaging
retaliated: struck back
ruthless: brutal or merciless
indefatigable: untiring
punitive: punishing

hurled through the air, crashing down through a power line that led from the generator to the rides at the amusement park. James rolled away from the electrical wires, which were sending **copious** sparks into the dry **dune** grass. A few moments later the acrid smell of smoke reached James's nostrils. But there was no way to quench the flames. His legs were like rubber beneath him. He fell to his knees in the soft sand, spent, as Adam leapt toward him and grabbed him by the hair.

"I always knew that I would get **restitution**," Adam snarled. "Although I have to admit that it was a lot easier than I thought."

James was choking on his own blood. "I should have killed you when I had the chance," he managed to get out. Gagging, he struggled to swallow the mouthful of thick liquid and went on, "When I found the girl in the white room . . . when I saw just how cruel you were . . ."

Adam stared at him for a moment, then started to laugh. "The girl? She wasn't even mine!"

James stared into Adam's dark eyes, now twinkling with **execrable** mirth. "You're lying," James spat.

Adam's eyes narrowed. "Am I?" he demanded. "I'm telling you," he repeated, his voice low and urgent, "she wasn't mine."

James's mind reeled as Adam tightened his hold on his hair. Adam pulled something from his pocket that gleamed silver in the moonlight. James felt strangely detached from what was happening, as if watching it all from a long way off.

"James!"

James heard the scream. He recognized that it was Victoria's voice and that it was full of anguish. Still, it didn't rouse him. He was **demoralized**. There was no hope now. . . .

"James!" Victoria screamed again, and suddenly the small brush fire behind him shot into the sky.

"James!" The fire had become a **conflagration**.

copious: numerous
dune: hill of sand
restitution: repayment
execrable: terrible or disgusting
demoralized: discouraged
conflagration: blaze

James turned his eyes from it immediately, but Adam kept staring. In a movement that was little more than reflex, James caught hold of Adam's arm and twisted it. The bone gave way with a **brittle** crack, and suddenly Adam was flat on his back.

James landed his boot squarely on Adam's wrist, but Adam shoved him backward. The flames were on one side and the electrical wires on the other, and it was the wires that James stumbled toward under this latest attack.

Adam stood, his arm dangling at an awkward angle, the bone threatening to poke through the skin of his forearm. Taking his arm in the opposite hand, he pushed the bone back into place. A moment later the bone had knit together, healing itself, and Adam leapt after James.

"No!" Victoria shouted, and the earth beneath their feet rumbled, then split. James staggered toward a wire and picked it up. He turned and thrust out the wire just as Adam regained his footing and lunged at him.

There was a **corrosive** stench and the sizzle of searing flesh as Adam was pounded with ten thousand volts of electricity. James jabbed the wire against Adam's chest even harder, unflinching as Adam let out an **immense** scream that crescendoed across the sky, then died away, **dissipating** on the salt breeze of the sea.

A moment later there was nothing left but a few dark ashes.

James turned and saw that Victoria had fallen, her ankle twisted into the crack in the earth that had been created by the mini-earthquake. James hurried toward her.

Victoria's eyes fluttered open as James slipped an arm beneath her shoulders. "James," she whispered, "he was hurting you. . . ."

"That's over now," James said quickly. "He was a murderer, Victoria. The Vampire Killer. And he would have killed us both if . . ." He didn't go on. Even the thought of what could have happened was **anathema.**

brittle: fragile or dry
corrosive: harsh, damaging (as of a chemical)
immense: enormous
dissipating: dissolving or fading
anathema: intensely disliked

Victoria nodded, then looked down at where her foot was caught in the small chasm. "What happened?" she asked feebly, her face lit with the orange glow from the nearby fire.

James shook his head. He couldn't exactly explain it—not perfectly, anyway. But he had some suspicions. He remembered back to the night of the Wiccan circle—how he felt the power of all things flowing through him—and wondered whether the magic of Wicca could have **augmented** Victoria's vampire powers. But there was no question that the fire had leapt out of control at her scream, just as the ground beneath their feet had opened up when James was about to be killed. "I don't know what happened," James admitted.

He bent down and lifted her gently from the crevasse, surprised at how light she felt in his arms. Victoria blinked up at him, and James leaned forward and kissed her. The feeling of her lips on his was like a promise. This was what he had wanted. True, it was a fate that he never would have chosen for her, but he could hardly say that he was sorry. Maybe this was a crime for which he could never be **exculpated.** *Fine,* James thought, *then let me be damned. . . .*

James wanted to go on kissing her forever, but he knew that they had to leave before the police arrived. They couldn't allow themselves to be detained for questioning. He tore his lips away from hers and turned toward the boardwalk.

And that was when he came face-to-face with Alistair Masterson.

augmented: increased **exculpated:** pardoned

Chapter Fourteen

"Hello, James," Alistair said smoothly.

For a moment James didn't reply—he was too shocked by the older gentleman's presence. It had been five years since James had seen Alistair, but if anything, the vampire looked younger than he had before. James's heart leapt in his chest. Alistair! The mentor whose troubling teachings had remained with James—even in Alistair's absence—for all of these years.

Alistair stood there, his expression dark and **formidable,** as unyielding as a Grecian **deity** holding a thunderbolt. And in fact, in that moment the **atmosphere** seemed to thicken, the clouds growing heavy, obscuring the stars above.

"I see you've made a friend," Alistair went on, gesturing toward Victoria.

Thunder rumbled on the horizon. The **contusions** on James's face throbbed as he asked, "What are you doing here?" For a moment hope surged in his chest. Had Alistair guessed at Adam's plan and come to stop him from attacking James?

Alistair clucked his tongue. "Really, James, what sort of **salutation** is that for one's benefactor?" He smiled. "It has taken me a long time to find you. And even longer for you to find me . . . given your . . . **exemplary** gifts."

There was something in Alistair's tone that made James wary, and the thrill he had felt upon seeing Alistair was instantly **tempered** with fear. James's eyes flickered toward Adam, and his hopes sank. He had killed another vampire. Had Alistair come to deliver some kind of judgment? "What do you want from me?" he asked.

"The same thing I've wanted all along," Alistair replied. "James,

formidable: fearsome or imposing
deity: god
atmosphere: air or environment
contusions: bruises
salutation: greeting
exemplary: excellent
tempered: balanced or moderated

sometimes you're insufferably slow." Alistair's teeth gleamed, luminous, in the dim light. "I want you to live in an **environment** in which you can **flourish,**" he whispered. "I want you to **exorcise** your demons and finish the training you started long ago."

"What's he talking about?" Victoria asked.

"You see, James," Alistair said, never losing his composure. "This moment is the **culmination** of years of work. Now you must come back with me."

James held his hand against his throbbing face. "I'm not coming back with you," he said. James thought of his mother and Adam, of their repeated advice for him to accept what he was. He was tired of hearing it.

"Really, James," Alistair said, his eye sparkling with a dangerous twinkle that James had never seen before. "I knew you were **perfidious,** but I never expected you to be rude."

That was enough for James. He remembered how he used to hold Alistair in such high esteem and nearly **scoffed** at his own naïveté. *They're all alike,* James thought bitterly. Without another word, James brushed past Alistair. But the older vampire leapt over James and stood in his path once again. With a **perfunctory** slap, he knocked Victoria from James's arms to the ground. Victoria let out a dull grunt, and her eyes closed.

"Victoria!" James shouted, but Alistair slashed at his face. James reeled.

Alistair thrust himself at James, knocking him to the ground. James kicked his feet at Alistair in an attempt to trip him, but the older vampire proved nimble and leapt aside. James hauled himself to his feet and ran at Alistair. They fell against the sand, and James crushed his knee against Alistair's chest.

"Do you want to kill me?" Alistair asked, the evil sparkle in his eye brightening. "Do you?"

The rage was blinding. *Yes,* James thought. He did want to kill

environment: setting or surroundings
flourish: thrive or prosper
exorcise: get rid of
culmination: conclusion or high point
perfidious: disloyal
scoffed: mocked
perfunctory: mechanical or unthinking

Alistair . . . but in a moment the feeling had passed. James swallowed hard and stood up. "No," James gasped.

"That was always the trouble with you," Alistair said, straightening his clothes. "You never could accept your feelings. Why can't you just admit the truth? You wanted to kill me. You would have enjoyed it—just as you enjoyed killing Adam!"

"Adam deserved to die," James shot back. "I was **avenging** countless deaths. He was the Vampire Killer."

"Was he?" Alistair asked, a small smile playing at the corners of his mouth. "I suppose you have some **incontrovertible** evidence on this point."

"No, I—" James stopped suddenly and studied Alistair's face.

"You've been having dreams," Alistair said simply. "Dreams of the guilty."

"Yes," James whispered.

"For years. Only with this killer you dreamed of the kills . . . ," Alistair went on. "Weren't they beautiful, James?"

Adam's words sounded in James's ears—*She wasn't mine!*

"Death can be so beautiful . . . ," Alistair went on.

"The girl in the white room," James said slowly.

"Yes," Alistair said, nodding. "You took her from me, and I knew why. It was only then that I truly understood your **aversion** to the kill. But I knew that I could change your mind. Vampires are only as good as the blood they drink, James. That's why we must feed on the young and the innocent. I knew you would learn that, in time."

"She was yours," James went on, his mind working slowly. He felt weak. All he wanted to do was lie down. "And Adam . . ."

"Ah, yes . . . ," Alistair went on. "Well, comfort yourself with the knowledge that he had outlived his usefulness, even though he wasn't the Vampire Killer."

It was you. James wasn't sure whether he spoke the words aloud or just thought them, but they hung in the air like a living thing.

avenging: getting even for

incontrovertible: solid or unquestionable

aversion: dislike or distaste

And then the next thought—*I killed the wrong man.*

"Yes, you did," Alistair confirmed. He grabbed James's shoulder and squeezed it. "And you enjoyed it," he said fiercely.

"No," James said.

"Admit it!" Alistair cried. "**Exult** in it! You enjoyed the kill, and there's no need to **curtail** the slayings."

"No!" James shouted, louder this time.

"You're **inexorable**," Alistair snarled. He shoved James backward toward a **promontory**, an outcropping of rock that led toward the sea. "Just like your father."

James frowned, bile rising in his throat. "You knew my father?" he asked, a strange sense of dread filling him.

Alistair nodded. "He was a lot like you, James. He wanted the gifts of being a vampire without having to pay the price. He was too weak to accept his destiny."

"You killed him," James said breathlessly.

"On the contrary," Alistair replied. "I'm the one who tried to keep him alive. The other vampires killed him because he was a threat to their way of life. I tried to stop them. . . ."

"I don't believe you."

"That doesn't change the truth, James. I loved your father, and I tried to help him. Just like I'm trying to help you now."

"You aren't trying to help me," James spat bitterly. "Why would you?"

"Because we're family, James," Alistair said slowly. "Your father was my brother."

James shook his head, backing away, even though he knew at once that it was true. No wonder Alistair knew Angelica. And there'd always been something familiar about Alistair, something that had triggered an old memory in James, one he couldn't name. James should have **surmised** the truth long ago.

"And now it's time for you to join me," Alistair said. "Just as your

exult: rejoice or take pride
curtail: hold back
inexorable: unstoppable
promontory: rock outcropping
surmised: guessed

father would have wanted."

Victoria let out a groan, coming back to consciousness.

"Your friend can come too," Alistair said in a mockery of **cordiality.** "It will be nice to have a young woman around the house again."

"What about Susan?" James demanded, afraid to know the answer.

Alistair **chortled.** "She tried to follow you, after a bit. You made quite an impression on her, dear James. Unfortunately, she didn't get very far."

There was a flash of lightning. The mist hung heavy over the sea.

"No!" James shouted, once again lunging at Alistair. But he was no match for the older vampire—his speed and strength were completely **inferior** to Alistair's. With a movement quicker than sight Alistair whipped around, bringing his leg out against James's. James fell backward into the sand, and Alistair dealt him a punishing blow to the stomach.

Dimly James could see Victoria stagger to her feet behind Alistair. James wanted to tell her to run, to hide, to do anything to get away from here. But he couldn't speak. Alistair kicked him again, and James felt the sickening crunch as one of his ribs broke in two. Alistair hit him with a **pertinacious** series of kicks, and James could do little more than groan. It was no use—Alistair's **arsenal** was infinitely greater than his own.

But just when the pain reached its **acme,** just as James was certain that he was Alistair's, the heavens tore open. Like the hand of God, a lightning bolt reached down from the sky, lighting up Alistair in a magnificent display of agony.

Alistair's face **distended,** and he let out an inhuman scream. A moment later he was pushed backward into the water by a **preternatural** gust of wind and swept away into the sea.

James struggled off the promontory just as the first raindrops began to fall and hurried to where Victoria lay, unconscious from the strain of what she'd just done. There was no doubt in James's

cordiality: warmth or friendliness
chortled: chuckled or snorted
inferior: less or worse than
pertinacious: persistent
arsenal: store or stockpile
acme: high point
distended: swelled or stretched
preternatural: exceeding what is natural

mind—she had caused that lightning bolt to fall. Her powers were **unassailable.**

James felt her neck for a pulse and found one—weak, but there. In a moment Victoria's eyes fluttered open. "James," she whispered.

"It's all right," James murmured.

"What—what am I?" Victoria asked.

James shook his head. "I'm not sure," he said honestly. She was a vampire, of course, but she was also something more. "I swear . . . I'll tell you everything I know. But not tonight." He looked down at her injured ankle. "Can you walk?"

"I don't think so."

"Try moving your foot," James suggested.

Victoria did, and her eyes widened in surprise. "It's better."

James nodded. Of course. Her wounds healed themselves. "Then we'd better go." He helped Victoria up.

She put her arm around him, and the two vampires walked gingerly forward through the night, mindless of the pouring rain.

unassailable: invincible

Epilogue

"Victoria," James murmured, stroking her cheek. "Victoria, the sun has gone down."

Her eyes slowly opened. For a moment, a look of confusion passed over her face as she came out of her deep sleep, but then she smiled her Mona Lisa smile, so familiar to James after the nearly six months they'd spent traveling the world together. As selfish as he knew it was, he lived for that smile. Although there was no peace emanating from her eyes at moments like this, there was a connection and a strong sense of need, which resonated very strongly in James's mind.

"Shall we take our evening promenade?" James asked.

"Yes, that sounds perfect," Victoria agreed. She stood and stretched, and James admired her lean muscles and the soft curve of her neck. It was such a relief to be able to be close to her and no longer ache from fear of hurting her.

James reached out and touched her shoulder, letting his fingertips trace her collarbone. Lifting her hand to cover his, James felt a sizzle of energy as their hands connected. He blinked, staring at their linked fingers. This wasn't the first time it had happened. Lately, they'd had several occasions where touching each other had seemed to cause some kind of electrical current. But Victoria wouldn't discuss it, and James sensed it was best to restrain himself from saying anything.

"Let's go outside," Victoria said. She clasped his hand more tightly, then gently let it go as she turned to the door of their hotel room.

James followed her out onto the Oregon beach, just a few steps from where they'd been staying for several weeks now. It was a shame to leave—James had really enjoyed the beautiful gothic coast. But it was his rule, after all, that they never stay in one place for too long. Too much risk of being found by the wrong people—both vampire and human.

They began to walk along the sand, side by side. "Tonight will be a full moon," Victoria said, looking up at the darkening sky. James glanced at the rolling waves of the Pacific ocean, mesmerized by the fierce tide. "I was thinking I might hunt . . . alone, tonight," she added.

James stopped, looking at her in surprise. "But we've talked about this," he said. "It's not right for you—it's better this way, believe me. I don't want you to have to take the first bite. Ever." He shuddered. "It's already an abomination that you are forced to . . . to drink, to sustain your life. But to hunt? No, I just won't allow it."

Victoria laughed, a harsh laugh. "James, what century do you think we're in? You won't allow it? Just because we're vampires doesn't mean we're suddenly in the Dark Ages."

"You don't know what you're saying," James insisted, his frustration building. "Can't you just trust me?"

Victoria met his gaze, her eyes smoldering. She leaned in close. "Can vampires really trust?" she asked, her voice low. "Or be trusted?"

She pulled back, and James felt something akin to a soft kick in his gut. He stood rooted to the spot while Victoria resumed walking, as he tried to understand what was happening. She was changing—something inside of her was *changing*.

Some strange instinct caused James to jerk his head up. His eyes took in the emerging moon, round and full and tinged with shades of yellow.

Panic came over him, and he jogged to catch up to Victoria. He grabbed her arm and swung her around to face him. "What is it—what's going on?" he demanded.

The fire that had filled her expression moments ago was gone, and she looked back at him with a mixture of fear and sadness in her hazel eyes. "I don't know," she said. "James, I feel something, but I'm not sure what it is. It's different than when I became—when Adam made me into this. It's something more."

"What?" James breathed.

Victoria turned to the ocean. She narrowed her eyes in concentration, and as he watched, the waves crested higher and higher, seeming to reach toward the sky. "Take my hand," she whispered. James swallowed, terrified. "Take it—now!" she hissed. James snatched her hand in his and clasped it tightly, feeling a surge of shocks pass through his entire body. Suddenly the waves were rushing toward them, the powerful ocean about to overcome them. But as he gripped Victoria's hand, the water stopped inches away from them, held back by some invisible force.

Victoria let out her breath, and the waves sighed back toward the sea. In seconds, the horizon looked exactly as it had moments ago.

"How did you . . . ?" he trailed off, looking at her in awe. After that fateful night with Alistair, James had pressed her to see what more she could do, convinced of his theory that her Wiccan experience had somehow enriched her new vampire nature. But Victoria had insisted that what she'd managed had been a fluke, some bizarre event made possible by the extreme emotions she was under as she made the Change. Since then, she'd resisted all of his pleas to explore the issue further.

Victoria leaned into James, suddenly weak, and he put his arm around her. "I think you were right about me," she said. "There's something—different about me."

"You're not any kind of *ordinary* vampire," he said. "I always felt that."

She shook her head and swallowed hard. "James, I'm scared. . . . Just promise that you won't leave me, " she said. "At least, not now. . . ."

"I promise," he said softly, folding her into a tight embrace against him. "Whatever comes next, we'll face it together."

James quickly took Victoria's chin in his hands, trying to turn her head to face him directly, so he could promise her, swear to her, that she could trust him, rely on him, eternally. But Victoria's face seemed almost frozen in place, her eyes fixated on something in the distance.

"Victoria," he said firmly. "Listen to me. I won't leave you. You and I . . . we're together . . . forever."

She turned around and looked up at him slowly, her eyes still abstracted with their unnatural gleam.

"Forever," she repeated. Her voice was low and thickened. "I've never realized . . . what a long time that is."

TEST PREPARATION GUIDES

The SparkNotes team figured it was time to cut standardized tests down to size. We've studied the tests for you, so that SparkNotes test prep guides are:

SMARTER

Packed with critical-thinking skills and test-taking strategies that will improve your score.

BETTER

Fully up to date, covering all new features of the tests, with study tips on every type of question.

FASTER

Our books cover exactly what you need to know for the test. No more, no less.